Table of Contents

CHAPTER ONE

"I don't know how she did it." I stare at my dark complected step sister, Pam, across the small table after sipping my black coffee. I look at her with a clueless expression and she smiles, "Oh yeah, I keep forgetting that you just moved here. I was talking about her… Mrs. Devul." Pam points quickly to a thin lady standing behind me facing the register and I turn around slightly to get a better look at her. She's a stunning 50-something year old black woman with gorgeous, silver hair pinned up neatly in a french roll. Still confused by Pam's point, I turn back around to face her.

"Pam, what are you talking about? You don't know how she did what?" Pam sits her colorful coffee mug down before leaning towards me from her side of the table. I lean in as well, making sure that I can hear whatever it is she's about to say.

"I don't know how she gave birth to four of the most beautiful men to ever walk the face of this Earth." I smack my full lips at her stupid statement before sitting back in my chair. I turn my mouth up disappointedly at her and she giggles.

"You're only looking at me like that because you've never seen her sons. I'm telling you, they're fine."

I shake my head at her simpleness and sip from my mug again. I swear, if it wasn't for my mom marrying her dad, I wouldn't even be seen in public with a female like her. I can't stand a woman that is so easily impressed by a man just because he looks good. A fine man comes a dime a dozen, especially where I'm from. I require a lot more than that to get my panties all in a bunch.

She smacks her lips at my lack of enthusiasm, "Ok. You can act that way if you want, but I'm telling you, they'll take your breath away. Once you lay eyes on one Devul brother-"

"Wait a minute. Their name is 'devil'?"

"Not like Lucifer devil, it's spelled differently, but the pronunciation is basically the same. And girl, believe me, it's definitely fitting."

"What do you mean by that?" I ask, finally showing some sort of interest in what she's saying.

"I've never had one personally, but I know a few that have, and they say that the way those men lay dick, it had to come straight from the devil himself." I snicker after her comment, feeling like I've just heard the cheesiest line ever repeated. She leans back in her chair as if she doesn't care if I take her seriously or not. We stare at each other for a few seconds before she takes a deep breath, "Ok. Don't believe me. But just know this, you've been warned."

***

We leave the tiny coffee shop and walk down the street towards our home. I walk past the small stores on the town's main strip and look inside of every window. The people that I make eye contact with all smile and throw their hands up in greeting. I speak back, feeling a little weirded out by how friendly everyone is around here.

I thought I was going to hate moving to a small town after being a city girl my whole life, but I have to admit, I like it here. It's a little slow and there's not much to do, but the people are nice and sweet to say the least. It's almost impossible to fathom the thought of people not locking their car or house doors. Leaving things unlocked was definitely something we couldn't do when mom and I lived in Detroit.

"Hey, Mr. Stanson! How are you?" Pam stops enthusiastically to converse with a handsome, light-skinned, middle-aged man standing by the barbershop. I stop as well, deciding to wait for her so that we can continue our journey home. He looks at her as if he's surprised to see her.

"Pamela… hey. How are you, young lady?" The guy acts weird, causing me to fold my arms curiously. His nervous eyes constantly survey the area.
What's this guy's deal?

"I'm doing well. I haven't seen you around here in a while. Where have you been hiding?" He swallows hard with discomfort at her inquiry.
I get the feeling that their relationship is a little more personal than what meets the eye.

"Ronald, honey. The barber is waiting for you. It's your turn." A chubby, brown-skinned woman appears from the doorway of the barbershop, staring in the direction of us. She looks surprised to see us talking to Mr. Stanson and walks our way, "Ronald, who are your friends?"

Ronald takes a deep breath before acknowledging her, "Baby, this is my student from Mercury High. Well, she used to be my student. She's all grown-up now." He lets out a nervous snicker and Pam appears offended. I touch her shoulder in an attempt to get her attention for a second.

Pam turns around to face me and I give her a look as if to tell her to maintain her cool. She reads my eyes and quickly changes her body language from offended to calm. She nods her head slightly before turning back around to face her old teacher and his wife, "Yes, I used to be Mr. Stanson's student a few years back. I was just saying hello. I haven't seen him since I graduated."

Mrs. Stanson steps closer to Pam, "Yeah. We've been gone for a few years now. We were having our first baby so we decided to move into the city. Greater medical care, more housing options, it was just better all around for our growing family. I'm sure once you get to that point in your life, you'll understand what I mean." Pam gets offended once again and I decide to intervene. I quickly step in front of her.

"Hello, Mr. and Mrs. Stanson. My name is Amber, and I'm Pam's stepsister. I just moved here from the city, so I totally understand what you mean. I do like it here, though." I smile warmly at the couple, making Mrs. Stanson smile at me as well. She gives me a more inviting look than she did Pam.

"Oh, really? Which city?"

"Detroit." Mrs. Stanson's face lights up.

"Oh! The Motor City! I have family not too far from Detroit. They're in Kalamazoo." Mrs. Stanson talks to me for a few more minutes, even after Ronald walked into the barbershop to get serviced. Pam stands there awkwardly, causing me to bring my chat with her ex's wife to an end.

"Well Mrs. Stanson, I really should be going. I promised my mom I'd be back in time to help her with dinner." Mrs. Stanson nods as if she understands.

"Aww, that's awfully sweet of you, and please, whenever you see me around, don't hesitate to call me Connie." I smile once more at her before walking away. Pam waves goodbye to Mrs. Stanson swiftly while following my lead. Pam loops her slim arm into mine as we put some distance between us and Mrs.Stanson.

She looks over at my medium brown face, "Was it really that obvious?" I shake my head yes before even looking back at her.

"Terribly." She makes an embarrassed face.

"I wonder if Mrs. Stanson could tell." I hump my shoulders slightly.

"I'm not sure, but if I were you, I would stay far away from Mr. Stanson."

CHAPTER TWO

I woke up an hour ago, but I still haven't gotten out of bed yet. I slowly scroll through my best friends' social media accounts and sigh to myself. Rochelle just posted a picture of her and the rest of our crew 22 hours ago. I stare at the photo longer than I should, feeling completely awful for not being there with them right now.

Rochelle towers over my other two friends in the photo just like she usually does, sporting her 32 inch, black weave and six inch stilettos. Her chocolate brown legs are so oily that the flash from the camera bounces off them distractingly. She's thin enough to be a model, but not so small that she looks hungry. She's the perfect size, even though she complains about her body every chance she gets.

I don't understand her sometimes.

Shay is a midget compared to Rochelle. She's barely five feet, but she never wears heels. She claims she doesn't like them, but everyone knows that her weight is the real reason why she won't wear them. She's a little on the heavier side just like her family is. She has a gorgeous light-brown face, though. She's the epitome of beauty. No one can deny that.

Now Tanisha, she falls smack dab in the middle of Rochelle and Shay. She's the average height for a female and she's neither small nor big. Her waist is tiny, but her ass is fat. Her body is so well-proportioned that she looks like the after picture on a plastic surgeon's advertisement poster. She knows she's flawless, and she dresses like she is. Sometimes, her outfits are a little inappropriate, but that never matters to her. One thing's for sure, you're going to see an uncomfortable amount of her caramel skin whether you like it or not.

Even though I like my new environment, I miss my childhood friends like crazy. This is the first summer we won't be spending together and I'm sick about it. Even though the four of us all went our separate ways after high school, we still made sure to link up every summer to have some good old-fashioned, old-school fun. Even when I started college, I made sure to attend local classes just so I could see my friends whenever I wanted. Now that I live 13 hours away from Detroit, there's no telling how long it's going to be before I see them again.

"Good morning, doll," my mom says, opening my room door after knocking one time. I stare at her lovely face as she approaches my bed.

"Morning, ma. How are you feeling today?" She sits her lean body at the foot of my queen-sized bed.

"I'm ok. Trying to get used to the absolute boredom associated with this place." I sit up against my white headboard and giggle.

"Aww naw, don't say that now! When you told me we'd be moving to this spec on the map, you said it would be quiet and I was the one that used the word 'boring'. I told you." She giggles as well while humping her shoulders at the same time.

"Yeah, well... I knew it was going to be slow, but I didn't think it would be this slow." I smile while shaking my head at her, "I'm serious! We've been here for three months and I've barely been out of this damn house." I lay my phone next to me and swing my feet over the side of the bed.

"That's because you don't have to leave. You don't even have to get a job, remember? Your husband is loaded!" I stand up to stretch, "You don't have to lie, ma. I know that's the real reason why you married him." My mom smacks her lips and I hurry past her just in case she tries to hit me. I turn to face her after she folds her arms, "I'm just playing. I know you love Craig."

"I do love Craig… and it doesn't hurt that he is a little wealthy." Mom and I both laugh while she stands up as well. I stare at my Coke bottle shape in my full-length mirror, "I actually came in here to ask you to go to the store for me. I want to have a barbecue tomorrow and I need a few more items." My mom pulls a list from her jean pocket and hands it to me.

"A few more items? Geez mom, this is half of the store." She smacks her lips, "And who's going to eat all of this food? Only four of us live here, but there's enough food on this list to feed the entire town." She smiles as if she's up to something and grabs my shoulders.

"Don't worry about all of that, doll. Just go to the store for me, please." I nod in agreement, even though I'm hella suspicious of this whole barbecue idea that came out of nowhere. She kisses me on the cheek before walking towards my room's exit, "Come downstairs for breakfast before you go. Pam is almost done cooking." I nod my head again as she disappears from my sight.

***

I walk down the first aisle of the only grocery store this town has. I look at my mom's list and get upset once I can't locate half of the things on the white sheet of paper. After almost an hour of aimlessly searching, I stop in the middle of aisle four and close my eyes. I let out a frustrating sigh, trying my best not to have a complete meltdown in this establishment.

"Excuse me, miss, are you OK?" I open my eyes to find a handsome fellow standing in front of me. His brown eyes watch me closely and I jump out of surprise.

"Umm, yeah, I'm- I'm good. I'm just having a hard time finding what I need in this store." A perfect smile appears on his toffee-colored face as he looks down at the list in my hand. He reaches for it.

"May I?" I hesitate. His eyes move from the list to mine and my breathing seizes. I hand him the list slowly and he glances at it. "OK, I can definitely help you with this. Some of these items they might not have, but I believe they have most of this stuff." He starts to walk and I follow him with my cart. I watch him in motion and bite my lip... *Damn... who is this man?*

He stops in front of the condiments and reaches for the barbecue sauce. "We don't have Sweet Baby Ray's here, but this brand is pretty good." He hands me a bottle of a brand I've never heard of before and I study it.

"I guess if you say it's good, then I'll just take your word for it." I grab two more bottles of the brand's different varieties and toss them in my nearly empty cart. He smiles before quickly reading over the list again. We start moving before he says another word.

"I can't help but to notice that I've never seen you around before. Did you just move here?" He stops and browses in front of another shelf. I watch his muscles flex in his tight white tee when he reaches up to grab something. I swallow the lust growing in my throat.

"Yeah, you can say that. I've been here for three months or so." He makes a shocked expression as he tosses more items into my cart.

"Wow, you've been here for three months and I've never seen you before? It sucks to be me." I blush immediately from his words but wipe the flattered expression off my face before he gets a chance to notice. I clear my throat.

"Yeah, this is a pretty small town. I'm sure everyone knows everyone." He glances at me with interested eyes and my heart rate speeds up. He looks me up and down slowly.

"Apparently not. I don't know you." I giggle nervously once he licks his lips. He steps closer to me, allowing his manly presence to dominate my feminine stature. "Let's fix that. Hi, my name is Danny, Danny Devul, and you are?" My eyes get big once he says his name. I can't believe that a day after hearing about the Devul brothers, I'm actually meeting one!
And Pam was right… he is fine.

"Hello, Danny Devul. It's nice to meet you. My name is Amber Morris." I stick my hand out for him to shake but he grabs me around my waist instead. He pulls me into him, forcing me to take in the scent of his seductive cologne.

"It's nice to meet you as well, Amber," he says in a low, sexy tone, causing my body to form chill bumps all over. "And sorry, but I'm a hugger." He loosens his grip and stares into my eyes, "Especially when a woman as beautiful as you is involved."

I fall into his gaze, forgetting where I am for a second. He caresses the small of my back and my pussy wakes up like someone has shouted its name. I take a step back before my underwear becomes drenched with my love juice.
For some reason, he seems like the kind of man that can smell horny on a woman.

"Umm, no need to apologize. Hugs are cool. I like hugs." I start rambling in a nervous tone and instantly get embarrassed. He observes the impact he has on me and smirks to himself.

"Good, because I'm hoping to get one every time I see you." My eyes get big with intrigue.
Every time he sees me?

I fight the giddiness expanding in my chest. We stand there until the atmosphere gets awkward. He looks at the list again, "Let me finish helping you with these items so that you can be on your way. By the looks of this list, you seem to be throwing some sort of party and I don't want to interrupt."

CHAPTER THREE

I bring the last of the plastic bags into the kitchen where Pam and my mom are already busy unpacking groceries. I sit the heavy items on the wide counter and sigh with relief.

"I'm glad you finally made it back. I was just about to send Pam up there to look for you," my mom states, staring at the strange bottles of barbecue sauce before placing them in the wooden cabinet. I lean against our marble kitchen island and fold my arms.

"I wish you would've sent Pam instead of me, period. I was having the hardest time finding anything in that store."

"Oh, I'm sorry, doll. I forgot that you really don't know your way around yet. It seems like you still managed to get most of the things on the list, though. Thank you for going." My mom's comment about her grocery list makes me think about Danny and I blush. Pam notices my change in facial expressions and stares at me curiously.

"Why the smile all of a sudden? What are you thinking about?" I hump my shoulders shyly before blushing again. Both my mom and Pam give me their undivided attention.

"Nothing really. I was having a hard time shopping, that was until I got a little help."

"Got a little help? Help from who?" I glance at my short mother after her questions and then at Pam. I give Pam a 'you know' type of look and her eyes widen.

"A Devul brother?" Pam inquires eagerly. I nod my head yes with excitement and she squeals.

"Wait a minute, who? The devil's brother?" My mom looks extremely frightened by Pam's question and Pam and I burst out laughing.

"No, mom! A Devul brother, like his last name is Devul." My mom's face is still traumatized.

"I don't know, doll; you may want to stay away from people with the last name 'devil'." Pam and I laugh again while shaking our heads. We get quiet for a few seconds, allowing mom a moment to comprehend what we're saying. She finally makes a face as if she gets it and I grin with amusement.

"So, tell me! Which one did you meet?" Pam asks while we continue to unpack the food. I set a few random products on the counter.

"Danny." Pam stops her movements and looks at me again.

"Danny?! Oh my gosh girl, he's so fine!" Pam's eyes roll upward with satisfaction at the thought of him, "He's the second youngest, too. He's around your age." I make a pleasantly surprised face, "Did you see any of the other Devuls?"

"Nope… and I'm glad I didn't, either. Danny was more than enough eye candy for me to handle." Pam giggles as if she knows exactly what I mean.

"What did I tell you yesterday? I tried to warn you! You thought I was playing, didn't you?" I roll my eyes at her while sporting a huge smile on my face. I reluctantly nod my head yes.

"I'm not going to lie, I did think you were overexaggerating, but girl, I'm so happy you weren't!" Pam and I giggle like school girls and my mom smacks her lips.

"Y'all need to cut it out. That boy can't be that fine." We both look at my mother like she's bugging. She looks taken aback,"Oh… well… excuse me!" We giggle even more, "Shit, I need to see this boy then! How about you invite him to the barbecue tomorrow? We'll have more than enough food." I look surprised by her unexpected invitation. So surprised, in fact, that I don't know what to say.

"Come on, sis. You should call and invite him. You do have his number, right?" I slowly shake my head no and both women look shockingly disappointed in me.

"You're telling me that you let him get away without getting his digits?" Pam shakes her head in disbelief. I hump my shoulders with embarrassment.

"I mean… I didn't want to look desperate. If he wanted to talk to me again, he would've asked me for mine." Pam sighs loudly before turning her back to me to tend to another bag of groceries. I stand there feeling awkward, "So, you really think I should've asked him?" My mom shakes her head yes, but Pam doesn't acknowledge me right away. She eventually turns around to face me after she finishes doing what she's doing.

"Of course you should have, but that doesn't matter now." I take a discouraging breath.
I knew I should have been more assertive!

"But don't worry about it. Lucky for you, I know where they hang out at. We'll just head up there after we finish helping ma with the groceries so that you can ask that man for his number."

***

Pam and I walk down a street I've never been down before and I sigh with nervousness. I notice that the people scattered around this area are more "hood" than any of the other people in town. Even though they seem a little sketchy, the sight of them makes me breathe a little better. *It's something about these folks that make me feel right at home.*

We walk past a few rundown restaurants that have some of the best smelling aromas I've ever inhaled in my life. I stop to stare inside of a few of them, pleased to see a big-boned, black woman standing behind most of their counters.

"Smells heavenly, doesn't it?" Pam asks after I stop to be nosy for the third time. I nod my head without even looking at her. "I know, right. Just be careful. I gained 20 pounds fucking with Mrs. B's food." She points at one of the ladies behind the counter and I grin. Mrs. B notices us watching her and waves in our direction. Pam and I wave back before continuing our walk.

"Well, here we are… Burton's Gym," Pam informs me as we approach an old building. I can tell that it said Burton's Gym once upon a time, but the letters are so worn out that it says " ton's ym" now.

"This is where all of the gorgeous men hang out. My friends and I used to ride up here when we were bored so that we could muscle-watch. Girl, on popular days, sitting out here was better than going to the movies." I shake my head at the thought of doing that thirsty shit, but then check myself immediately.
Your ass is up here on a thirsty mission as we speak, so you can't judge anyone, Amber.

Pam leads me to the front door and we walk in. I spot a small desk up front, but there's no one behind it to greet us. The sound of weights clinking makes my nervousness come back, reminding me quickly of what I came up here to do. Danny is probably somewhere in this place at this very moment and I'm about to approach him like a stalker.
I hope he doesn't think I'm completely insane for doing this crazy shit.

We turn a corner and I stop once I see all of the men on the huge gym floor working out. I blink in slow motion while trying to process the sea of sweat-covered bodies. My mind is overloaded with physical pleasure. I've never seen this many buff men at one time in my life!

"A lot to take in, I know, but come on. The Devuls are usually over there in that area." Pam grabs my hand after pointing at the furthest corner from us and tugs me down the gym's narrow pathway. The random men are so busy tackling the heavy equipment that they barely notice us walking past them. I gawk at each one, taking in the godliness of their builds. I stare at their pectorals and glutes until Pam speaks again.

"Oh my, I've spotted the big Devul." She lustfully fans herself before pointing inconspicuously and I follow her finger. I see a chocolate fellow holding hand weights and my mouth falls open. His flawless body drips with perspiration as he does rep after rep. He stares at his biceps flexing until he's satisfied with his count.

"Girl…" is all I can say, watching him like he's a piece of expensive ass art come to life. I shake my head slowly in disbelief.

"Sis, that's Richie, the oldest of the brothers. He's so laid back and mature, like you can lay your head on his strong ass shoulder and talk to him all night long." Pam shakes her head wishfully at the thought and I giggle. She regains her composure right before another guy appears near Richie.

"What?! Oh my God!" I perk up from her reaction, trying to figure out what she sees that has her so animated. She turns her tall body towards me excitedly, "Girl! That's Bruno, the second oldest Devul!" I would be embarrassed by her eager tone if it wasn't so noisy in this gym. I stare at her confusedly, prompting her to explain herself.

"Sorry, I keep forgetting that you're not from here!" She stomps with frustration before clearing her throat, "Bruno is always in and out of trouble. The last time he did something illegal, he went to prison for it. I thought he was going to be locked up forever. I haven't seen him in like five years! I can't wait to tell my girls that Bruno's out! They won't believe it!" I nod my head as if I understand, even though I don't fully comprehend her weird obsession with these men. You would think they were celebrities or something by the way she talks about them.

I turn away from her to stare in the direction of Richie and Bruno again. Now that she mentions it, Bruno does look like he's spent some time behind bars. He's a little taller than Richie and sports muscles and tattoos that look like they came straight from the cellblock. He has this ora about him, like he's not to be fucked with. That's usually not my type, but my homegirls would love him. *Damn, I miss my friends!*

"Wait, so who is that?" I point at another guy walking from the bathroom and Pam stares to see who I'm talking about. Even though he's nowhere near Richie and Bruno, he still looks like he can be related to them. She smiles widely when she notices who I'm referring to. She places her arm around my shoulders.

"Sis, now that right there is a god." She talks like he's famous and I chuckle.
He is delicious-looking, but he's no Michael B. Jordan.
I shake my head and she smacks her lips, "Amber, do you not see him? That's the baby Devul himself! Gosh, that man is perfect!" She squeezes me tightly as if she's imagining I'm him and I forcefully free myself from her hold. She snaps back into reality with an embarrassed giggle, "Oops, my bad." I shake my head and laugh at her. We stare back in the direction of the youngest Devul, "Girl, his name is Dame and he graduated when I did. I had to drool over that man for four years-"

"Why didn't you ever say anything to him?" Pam looks a little perplexed by the question.

"I mean, I did! But not about me liking him or anything like that. Him and I were actually pretty good friends in high school. Now, we only talk whenever we run into each other, which unfortunately, ain't that often."

"So, why not change the narrative-"

"Hey, Amber Morris!" A man grabs me from behind and hugs my waist tightly. I spin around quickly, looking like I'm ready to kick his ass. Danny notices my facial expression and takes a swift step back, "Shit! My fault. I didn't mean to scare you." My face softens up at the sight of him and I blush. He smiles as well, "Seriously, I'm sorry if I offended you. I told you that I wanted a hug every time I saw you, so I came to collect." He sticks his arms out and I don't hesitate to get in between them. He hugs me like we've known each other forever, making Pam's face hit the floor from our interaction. We finally separate.

"So, what brings you to the gym?" He looks me up and down lustfully, "A body as beautiful as yours needs no manipulation." I cheese uncomfortably hard and Pam elbows me. I can tell she's trying her best not to squeal with excitement.

Hell, she and I both.

"Actually, I was up here looking for you. You didn't bring up my phone number the last time I saw you, so I wanted to give you another chance to ask for it." I flirt with him with my almond-shaped eyes and he licks his lips. He steps ridiculously close to me.

"Oh, really? You want me to have your number?" His chiseled, shirtless body tries to distract me, but I maintain our eye contact. I smirk at his antics.

"Only if you'll use it." He smirks back.

"How about this, I'll give you my number and you can use it whenever you're ready to see me again." We take turns placing the ball in each other's court. I shake my head slightly at the games.

"Evidently, I was ready to see you again. I found you, remember?" He nods his head with flattery, "And on top of that, I want to see you tomorrow, too. My mom is throwing a barbecue, and I want you to be there." He smiles for a moment before digging in his pocket and pulling out his phone. He unlocks it and hands it to me.

"Here. Lock your number in, and I'll call you later on tonight so that we can fall asleep on the phone together."

CHAPTER FOUR

"Did you really talk to Danny all night?" I blush at Pam's inquiry while cleaning the collard greens in the sink. I nod my head yes to answer her question. She makes a shocked and slightly jealous expression, "Wow, I thought he was bullshitting."

"Girl, so did I." Pam dices up celery for the potato salad.

"So, what did y'all talk about?"

"Some of everything. Apparently, he's never been to Detroit before so he wanted to hear all about Motown. He's really into music." Pam makes a face as if she had no idea. I continue, "We talked about our childhoods for a while. Nothing too personal, just the basics. He talked a lot about his brothers, too. Evidently, they're a very close family. It's rare to see that nowadays." I get silent as the conversation with Pam causes me to relive the six hour cake-session I had with Danny last night. I can't believe how easy it was to open up to him. It's like everything flowed so naturally. I haven't felt that way about a guy since I met my first love, Dwayne. That was almost a decade ago, though.

"So, is he coming to the barbecue?" I smile at her question.

"Of course he is. He loves to eat. I found that out about him, too."

Pam makes a curious face, "You almost sound like y'all are in a relationship already." I grin to myself before humping my shoulders.

"Naw, we're simply getting to know each other better. We're just friends."

"Well, look at who I found at the bus station this morning," I hear my mom say from behind me. I turn around to see who she's talking about.

"Oh my God! Girls!" I scream, running over to my three best friends for an emotional group hug. We hold each other and rock from side to side. "You bitches! Why didn't you tell me you were coming?!" I shout out while forgetting that my mom is standing there. She places her hand on her hip and I cover my mouth quickly. "Sorry, ma. It slipped."

My mom giggles and shakes her head, "Ok nah, just don't let it slip again." My friends and I laugh at her before turning our attention back to one another.

"Oh my gosh! Shay, Rochelle, Tanisha! It's so good to see you chicks!" We all hug each other again excitedly.

"I know, right! It was so hard for me to keep this secret from you. That's why I haven't called you in two weeks. Ever since the girls and I came up with the idea, I've been trying my best to hold the surprise," Rochelle admits with the other ladies nodding their heads in agreement.

I smile at her, "I was wondering why you weren't answering the phone. Tanisha said you met a new dude, so I figured you were busy laying up with him." Rochelle elbows Tanisha and Tanisha giggles.

"Hey, I had to come up with something! And don't act like it's unheard of for you to meet a guy and then disappear for a while." Rochelle smacks her lips and we all snicker.

Shay shakes her head at us, "See ladies, just like old times." We all laugh at her sarcasm. I turn around and see

Pam staring nosily at us. I call her over to where my friends and I are standing.

"Girls, I want you to meet my stepsister, Pam." Everyone gives her a dry hi and Pam smiles awkwardly at them. We stand there with a lingering silence that gets uncomfortable quickly.

"Uh, Amber has told me a lot about you. I feel like I know all of you even though we've never met." Pam giggles uncomfortably and the girls stare at her challengingly. I put my arm around Pam's shoulders.

"Pam has been so good to me while I've been here. Without her, I'd be bored out of my mind." I try to hint to my good friends that it's OK for them to put their guards down when it comes to Pam. Shay is the only one that picks up on it...

Or wants to for that matter.

"Ok, that's cool. It's nice to meet you, Pam. What were you over there doing?"

"Cutting up celery," Pam answers quickly, feeling slightly relieved that someone is trying to be friendly with her.

Shay continues with her questioning, "Oh, OK. What are you using the celery for?"

"My potato salad. I'm telling you, it's to die for." Shay smiles at Pam's confidence.

"I'll be the judge of that because I love potato salad! But in the meantime, I'll help you." Shay and Pam grin warmly at each other. Shay follows Pam over to the kitchen island where Pam was preparing her vegetables and they start talking amongst themselves. I gawk at Tanisha and Rochelle watching Shay and Pam until I clear my throat to get their attention. They stare at me with unpleasant looks on their faces. I smack my lips.

"Stop it!" I whisper while stepping closer to them. They both glance at me blankly, "I'm serious! Don't treat her like that. She's nice!"

Rochelle turns her big lips up and folds her arms, "Mm. Well, I don't know her-"

"Me, neither." Tanisha co-signs, "Plus, you told us that you don't like her like that anyway."
Damn! I did say that, didn't I? Me and my big, fat mouth.

"Well, that was how I felt when I first got here. We're getting along much better now. So please, just try… for me." They both sigh heavily before reluctantly okaying my request. I smile gratefully at them. I head over towards my sink of greens. I glance at them, then check the stock pot on the stove that's boiling the turkey tails and onions. Rochelle peeks in the pot with me.

"Girl, you know I love your greens." I look back at her long face.

"I know. Do me a favor and put those collards in here. I need to start seasoning the meat."

"Amber, you know I can do that. Just let me wash my hands first, and then point me in the direction of the seasonings," Tanisha jumps in, offering her assistance. She walks over to Rochelle and I.

"Ladies, I'll show you where you're sleeping, then I'll show you where the bathrooms are. After that, we can all come back in here and throw down like we used to do," my mom says from the background. The ladies look at her lovingly before following her down the hallway.

Pam joins me at the stove, "They seem nice." I glance back at her as if to say, "yeah right" and she laughs at my facial expression.

"They aren't, but I'll get them there. Don't worry about it."

***

I sit in our huge backyard and watch Craig cooking on the grill. My mom walks up to her older husband, whispers something in his ear, and then kisses him on the cheek. I smile to myself at the thought of my mom being in love. After all she's been through with my dad and other men, she definitely deserves it.

"Aww, your mom looks so happy," Shay points out, taking the thought straight from my mind. I look at my girls sitting around the glass patio table before responding.

"She is, and I'm so glad, too. It's been a long time since I've seen her smile this much." Rochelle looks around our huge backyard before looking back at me.

"I'd smile, too, if I had a pool with a damn waterfall over it." I laugh at her statement, "I'm serious! Look at this shit! I've only seen things like this in the movies-"

"Same here," Tanisha agrees. I hump my shoulders slightly.

"I feel you. I was a little taken aback when I moved here myself. Coming from a small, two bedroom ranch in Detroit to a damn mini-mansion in Georgia, it took some time to get used to. Hell, I'm still not fully used to it yet."

Rochelle throws her long hair behind her shoulder, "Well, I could get used to it… quickly."

I shake my head at her, "Of course you could."

We sip our cocktails and the table gets quiet.

"You didn't need to make this drastic ass change in the first place," Tanisha mumbles, breaking the silence between us. I look at her strangely.

"What did you say?" Shay and Rochelle both look at Tanisha as if they want her to refrain from repeating herself. She ignores their glares and folds her arms.

"Don't ask me what I said like you didn't hear me. You know exactly what I said." I make a shocked facial expression.

"Wow," is the only word I can think of, folding my arms as well. Shay looks at the both of us worriedly.

"Amber, Tanisha didn't mean anything by that. She means well… really. It's just that we were all having a conversation one day about you moving here with your mom-"

"Hold up, y'all been talking about me behind my back?" I cut Shay off to ask after my 'turn-up button' gets activated. Rochelle jumps in quickly.

"Amber… come on, girl, you know it's not like that. It's all love all the time and you know that."

"So, what did Tanisha mean, then? Why would she say that?"

"Because it's true," Tanisha blurts out, causing me to direct my death ray stares back at her. "You're a grown ass woman, Amber. You didn't have to move so fucking far away with your mom. So what, you couldn't finish school. And? You still could've stayed in the 'D' and moved in with one of us. We would've figured something out-"

"Like what, Nish? Like me mooching off of y'all until I could find a low-paying ass job? All of y'all graduated college and got great jobs, and I couldn't even get past my second year in community college! I felt like a fucking failure!"

"Amber, calm down, it's alright-"

"No, it's not alright, Shay! There was nothing left in Detroit for me! I needed to get away from that place… I needed to get away from everything-"

"Yeah, including us!" We all abruptly get quiet once we realize that everyone is staring at us while we shout at one another. We sink down in our chairs with embarrassment. My mom walks over to our table.

"Ladies, is everything OK over here?"

"Yeah, mom. Sorry, we just got a little carried away, that's all." She looks at all of us sternly.

"Mmhmm… that better be all it is." We sit there feeling like awkward, small children. Mom places her hand on her hip, "Get it together. The food is almost ready."

CHAPTER FIVE

I sit at a table talking to Pam while my friends sit at the table I left them at right after our heated argument. Even though I told my mom that everything was alright, I still felt a certain way about them talking about my misfortunes behind my back. For the first time ever, I don't feel like I'm a part of our group anymore.

I guess me moving away showed their true colors.

"So, where's Danny?" Pam asks, trying her best to save me from my thoughts. She sips from her ginger ale. I hump my shoulders quickly.

"Hell, I have no idea. The last time I heard from him was last night. I texted him today to let him know what time everything was starting but he never responded."

"Well… maybe something came up and he couldn't make it." I pick my phone up to make sure he hasn't tried to contact me...

He hasn't.

I sigh.

"Yeah… maybe. But I would hope that if that would've been the case, he would've told me that. This no call, no show shit ain't-"

"Doll, you have guests." Pam and I both look towards ma quickly as she walks from the side of the house with a huge smile on her face. She winks in our direction as we see Danny and his brothers following closely behind her.

Gasp!
Every woman in the backyard stops breathing when the Devul brothers come into view. They are all dressed simply, sporting nice jeans and fitted tees. They stroll with confidence like their dicks are made of gold and my pussy jumps for joy. Danny smiles when his eyes catch mine. I blush uncontrollably from the sight of him.

"I'm assuming that one of these gentlemen is Danny," mom blurts out as soon as she reaches our table. Shay, Tanisha, and Rochelle get up from their seats and move closer to where Pam and I are sitting.

"Yes ma'am, that'll be me. It's nice to meet you. Amber didn't tell me that she had another sister." My mother blushes at Danny's attempt to impress her while I shake my head at his cheesiness. His brother, Dame, shakes his head as well and I snicker.

"Oh hush, doll! I do look young enough to be your sister! But no, I'm her mother. It's nice to meet you as well, Danny." Mom glances at his brothers, "And who are these other gentlemen?"

"These are my brothers… Richard, Brunard, and Damien. They weren't planning on staying, I just wanted to introduce them to your beautiful daughter." My mom tries not to stare at the Devuls, but she can't help herself. I don't blame her, either.
The sight of them is definitely too amazing to turn away from.

"Oh, nonsense! They can stay if they'd like! It's plenty of food." Mother points to the table of prepared dishes and Bruno rubs his hands together. Danny looks back at his brothers.

"So, what y'all wanna do?"

"I'm staying," Bruno says quickly, eyeballing the food like he hasn't eaten all day. Dame looks in the direction of us ladies and bites his bottom lip.

"I'm staying, too." The girls giggle with giddiness except for Pam. Pam just stares at him with a starstruck look in her eyes.

"If it's not too much trouble ma'am, we'll all stay," Richie adds with a voice as deep as the ocean is vast. It catches us all off guard, causing everyone's panties to disintegrate into thin air immediately.

"Well, it's settled then. Please make yourselves at home. There's a bathroom in the pool house if you want to wash your hands. Food is over there, drinks are in the cooler." The Devuls thank my mom for her hospitality before she rejoins Craig at the grill. The brothers head towards the beach house and Rochelle, Shay, and Tanisha hurriedly sit down at the table with Pam and I.

"Girl! Who the fuck?!" Rochelle asks before anyone gets a chance to say a word. My friends gawk at me impatiently.

"Those are the Devuls, "I pause when their gorgeousness crosses my mind, "I've been getting to know Danny recently, so I invited him to the barbecue. I had no idea he'd bring his brothers, though."

"Hell, I'm glad he did!" Tanisha blurts out thirstily. "What about that Dame one? He is highly fuckable," she adds, making Pam look at her territorially. Tanisha notices her glares and speaks up quickly, "Oh, my bad. I didn't know that was you, sis." Pam retracts her expression with a disagreeing gesture.

"No, he and I aren't dating or anything like that. He's just my friend." Pam looks away awkwardly with her correction as if she didn't want to admit that. Tanisha smirks at her confession and I narrow my eyes at her.

"Damn, Tanisha! Chill! We just got here two minutes ago and you're already trying to bounce on some dick," Shay exclaims with a disgusted look on her face. Tanisha smacks her lips at her.

"Oh, shut up, Shay! I'm on vacation, so I'm going to enjoy myself. I suggest you do the same."

The men walk out of the pool house and Tanisha rapidly stands to her feet. She hikes up her already short red dress until it rests right underneath her big ass cheeks. Her thick thighs catch Dame's attention immediately, causing him to lick his lips seductively. He looks her up and down before making intense eye contact with her.

"Fellas, I want y'all to meet my new special friend, Amber," Danny expresses to his brothers once they make it back to our table. My flattered feelings radiate from my smile as they each speak to me one by one. Rochelle nudges me under the table in an attempt to rush my introduction of her. I cut my eyes her way before speaking up.

"And guys, I want y'all to meet my friends Rochelle, Tanisha, and Shay," I point to each one as I say their names, "And I'm sure you already know my sister, Pam." I drop Pam's name last and she throws her hand up at the men. They acknowledge her quickly before turning their attention back to me and my friends.

"So, where are you ladies from?" Richie asks with enough bass in his voice to vibrate our clits. We adjust our pussies in our seats once they get warm.

"Umm, Detroit," I answer, trying to play it off like his voice has no effect on me whatsoever. He nods his head at my answer.

"What about you fellas, were you born and raised here?" Rochelle inquires, interjecting herself into the conversation.

"Yeah. We've been here our whole lives-"

"Most of us, anyway," Dame interrupts, cutting Richie off while staring at Bruno. Bruno gives Dame an evil glare before nudging him hard in the arm. Richie and Danny both shake their heads at their childish moment.

"Well damn. I guess Amber had the right idea by moving here, then," Tanisha says without taking her eyes off of Dame. They flirt hard with each other from a distance. I roll my eyes at her whorish ways.
Let a guy earn the coochie for a change.

"Sorry, we're being rude. Would you guys like to sit down," I offer, pointing at the empty seats around the nice-sized table. Each one of them grabs a chair and eases into it. Tanisha strategically plants her ass next to Damien. He watches her cheeks fall from underneath her dress as she exaggerates her way into the sitting space.

We all stare at each other's faces, secretly choosing the one that best fits our desires physically. Danny and I make eye contact and blush uncontrollably at one another. The quietness lingers, but our eyes speak for themselves. Pam is able to catch Dame's attention for a moment, that is until Tanisha brushes her shoulder against his. He looks over at her and she whispers something in his ear. They both chuckle, making Pam fold her arms with envy. Tanisha playfully bumps into him again before acknowledging everyone at the table, "How about some drinks? It's time to get this party started."

CHAPTER SIX

"I didn't know your friends would be here," Danny states after we finally find a small table where we can be alone. I sip my drink before looking over at him.

"Me, neither. Apparently, the girls and my mom came up with the idea. It was a surprise." I sigh after my words. Danny looks at me curiously.

"Well, you don't seem too happy about it." I hump my shoulders as if I'm not sure.

"Didn't you just tell me last night that you missed the shit out of your friends?"

"Yeah… I did."

"So, what happened between last night and today?" I stare down at the green straw resting in my glass as if the question he just asked me was a difficult one. He sits back in his chair after grabbing his own drink.

"My bad if that was too personal-"

"It's not that," I correct him quickly. We make eye contact and my skin gets tingly from his gaze.

"It's like, since they've been here, I've felt like… well…"

"Like you're out of place with them?" He hits the nail right on the head. I look shocked by his ability to know that. He puts his arm around my chair.

"Yeah, but… How did you know?" He sighs and I scoot my body closer to his. His arm falls around my shoulder.

"Because, I've been there before. When you live in a small town, it seems like the dream for most people is to graduate and get the fuck out of here, like this place is a disease or something. My best friends couldn't wait to leave. They left the summer after graduation and moved into the city. Even though they're not that far away, we still don't hang out much anymore. Now, everytime I see them, I feel like a stranger. They're talking about shit that I can't relate to, going places that I've never been to before. I mean, I get it, but still…" I nod my head at him as if I understand what he means, even though my situation isn't that severe.

It may be that way in another year or two, though.

"I don't know. I guess I feel like they're secretly holding a grudge against me for moving away, but there was nothing left in Detroit for me. I was beginning to get depressed. I needed a new environment. Plus, I wasn't just gonna let my mom move this far away by herself. I mean, I know Craig, but I don't KNOW Craig-"

"And don't forget, if you never would've come, you never would've met me." Danny speaks in a tone that awakens my soul. I make eye contact with him and instantly notice the passion in his eyes. He moves his lips slowly towards mine, licking them before he presses them…

"You're really about to make out with ma over there watching?" Danny and I separate quickly when we hear Pam's voice. She points to momma and I spot her eyeing me like a hawk. I frown up at her "black mom moment", shaking my head so that she can see me. She waves the spatula in our direction in a scolding manner before looking down at the grill.

"I think ma keeps forgetting I'm grown as hell," I mumble, completely irritated that she extinguished the fire that was burning between Danny and I.

"Tell me about it. I know that feeling all too well. That's just the pros and cons of living with moms." Danny stands to his feet with his words in an attempt to put a little distance between us and I huff disheartenedly. He looks around curiously, "Has anyone seen Dame?" Pam smacks her lips at the question.

"Yeah, I did, when he was walking towards the pool house with Tanisha about 15 minutes ago." Danny and I both look at each other before heading that way. Pam stands still for a few more seconds, deciding to tail us at the last minute.

We walk inside and find the place empty. We stand in the middle of the pool house's lounge space for a moment, wondering where they both could have gone. We remain quiet until we hear peculiar noises coming from the bathroom. Danny and I look at each other.

"No!" I whisper to him with widened eyes. He shakes his head disappointedly.

"Hell yeah, especially when it comes to Dame's perverted ass." Pam's face becomes covered with grief. My heart secretly aches for her.

Danny places his finger over his lips as he tiptoes towards the bathroom door. He places his ear against it before opening the door slowly. He peeks in and makes an alarming face. He signals for us to join him, but Pam denies the visual and leaves the pool house entirely. Danny steps to the side and I take a look.

My eyes get wider once I see Tanisha perched on her knees in front of Damien. Her mouth slides sloppily up and down Dame's hard dick. She slurps on the chocolate, veiny meat, impressively taking the majority of its length down her throat without gagging. Dame makes a face of astonishing pleasure while holding a fistful of Tanisha's curly weave. He fucks her face aggressively, making my clit throb from the explicit live action.

"Oh yeah, baby… yeah. I'm gonna cum in your mouth," Dame grunts out between labored breaths. Tanisha doesn't react negatively to the news. Instead, she sucks his thick penis more intensely. He releases her hair and grabs the sink behind him. His chest vibrates with broken heaves right before he explodes all over her tongue. "Shit, baby!" He exclaims, looking down at her like she just did him a great service. She swallows his load as I take a step back from the door.

"I can't believe her," I whisper to Danny, prompting him to look again. He shakes his head after glancing through the crack for a few seconds.

"Dame just looked up at me and smiled. I knew he knew we were watching. He's such an asshole." He walks towards the pool house exit, "Come on, let's get out of here. Your girl just got off the floor. They'll be coming out any minute."

CHAPTER SEVEN

I sit on the pool house couch next to Shay while Rochelle and Tanisha stand in the bathroom admiring themselves. Tanisha fixes her green thong swimsuit in the mirror and I secretly roll my eyes at her. This bitch has been here for less than 12 hours and she's already got more play than I have. Who sucks a dick without getting anything in return, though?

That's hoe shit.

"Amber, what's been going on with you?" Shay asks, staring at me with concerned eyes. I look over at her pie face and smile.

"Nothing. Why do you ask?"

"Because, ever since the guys left to get their swimming trunks, you haven't said two words." I hump my shoulders at her statement, trying to think of a reply. I shake my head as if I don't know what she means.

"Well, you know if there is something wrong, you can talk to me, right?" I nod my head yes and smile at Shay again.

Out of all my friends, she's the most caring.

"I do love your swimsuit, though. That orange is so cute on you," I state to change the subject. I glance down at her one piece, plus-size garment. She looks down at it as well.

"Thanks. It was expensive as hell! I need to lose some weight, shit. I can't afford to be this big for too much longer." I laugh at her and she giggles, too. Rochelle hears our good time and peeks out of the bathroom door.

"What's so funny?"

"Nothing. Shay is just crazy." Rochelle shakes her head amusingly at my answer as if she knows what I mean. Tanisha bumps past Rochelle and puts her back to us.

"How do I look?" She questions, clapping her ass in our direction. Shay and I both ball our faces up at her jiggling cheeks.

"You look like you're ready to bust it open," Shay responds, still displaying the same fucked up facial expression. Tanisha shakes her butt a little longer before turning around to face us.

"Good, because I definitely am." She sticks her tongue out freakily and I shake my head at her.
I want to keep my comments to myself, but fuck it…

"Put your damn tongue back in your mouth. Didn't Dame cum on it enough earlier today?" Rochelle and Shay both make a shocked face as all eyes zoom in on Tanisha. She places her hands on her wide hips.

"No the fuck he didn't cum enough, actually. And what's it to you? How do you even know about what happened between me and Dame anyway?"

"Because y'all didn't have the decency to take y'all ass somewhere private. Y'all had to do that shit a few feet away from a backyard full of people." Tanisha frowns her face up at me.

"Wait a damn minute… Tanisha… I know you ain't out here sucking random men's dicks?" She cuts her eyes at Rochelle after her question.

"I'm confused about what my mouth has to do with any of you bitches." We all shake our heads at her ignorant response as she continues, "And Amber, you sounding real mad, sis. What's the matter? You angry that I got more action than you and I just got here?" Tanisha calls me out perfectly and I stand to my feet. I take a few steps towards her.

"First of all, it ain't hard to get dick when you're a hoe. And secondly, I ain't letting nan motherfucka bust in my mouth without getting anything in return. I mean, who does that? I hope you got your 40, sis." Tanisha gets angry and comes towards me. Rochelle steps in between us right on time.

"Come on, girls. We didn't ride on that stankin' ass bus for 13 hours just to get down here and fight. We're better than that. Stop it." Tanisha rolls her eyes at me before turning around and heading towards the pool house door.

"Yeah, whatever. Say what y'all want, but I'ma get it in whether y'all like it or not."

***

"Shit," Shay mumbles under her breath once we spot the Devul brothers walking towards us. Even though it's a dark night, we can still see their buff, shirtless bodies glistening perfectly underneath the moonlight. Their swim trunks sit low on their pelvises, revealing their perfect 'V' cuts. I lick my lips at the sight of Danny's.
Maybe Tanisha is right. Maybe getting it in ain't such a bad idea after all.

"Ladies, sorry to keep y'all waiting, but something came up with moms," Danny mentions as soon as they get within our ear range. He walks straight up to me and embraces me tightly. "Mm, there's my hug," he whispers and his breath tickles my neck. Chill bumps form all over my skin. He kisses my shoulder before we separate. "You look so fucking sexy in your two piece, baby. You put that on for me?"
Oh, I'm his baby now?

"Umm, well, yeah… I guess. I just threw on the first swimsuit I could find. Nothing special." He looks me up and down with his mouth open in awe.

"Oh please believe me, baby. It *is* special."

"Damn, girl! You got all that ass out tonight, huh?" Dame asks Tanisha before grabbing a handful of it. She bounces it a few times and he slaps it.

"Yup, I shole do! You like it?" He bends down and bites one of her cheeks.

"I love it." She giggles and wraps her arms around his neck once he stands up in front of her. He palms her ass with both hands, tonguing her down nastily as if no one else is around. She slides her fingers down his washboard abs towards the top of his red trunks. She sticks her hand inside of them, stroking his long dick slowly.

He moans out loud enough for us to hear, "Damn, baby? Round two?" She nods her head yes lustfully. He takes her by the hand and leads her to the pool house again. Everyone stares inquisitively in their direction before finally deciding to mind their own business.

Richie greets Shay respectfully and she sparkles with flatteredness. He compliments her swimsuit, saying almost the same thing I said to her earlier about the orange garment.

"So, do you swim?" His voice roars through the backyard like the king of the jungle. Shay giggles nervously.

"Like a whale," she answers, choosing to make fun of her size before anyone else does.

Richie looks at her seriously, "I hope you don't think that's a bad thing. I love chewing on whale blubber." Rochelle and I both look at each other with saucer-shaped eyes before looking back at Shay. Her face lights up with intrigue. He takes her by the hand and they get in the pool together. He wraps his strong arms around her healthy waist immediately.

Bruno walks up to Rochelle and they greet each other in a timid fashion.

"You want a drink?" Rochelle questions Bruno in an uncomfortable voice. He nods his head yes without saying a word. Rochelle heads to the cooler and grabs a couple of beers. They sit at a table in the distance where they finally open up to each other a little more. I watch them interacting until Danny reclaims my attention.

"So, where's your mom and stepdad?" He inquires, grabbing my hand and leading me towards a chair. He sits down and tugs me down on his lap.

"Umm, they went to bed early. I guess all of that cooking tired them out." He licks his lips sexily after realizing that the party poopers are gone. I swallow with nervousness.

"And Pam, where's she?" I sigh at the thought of my upset stepsister.

"She went to bed early, too," I say, refraining from giving him details about her crush on Dame or her hurt feelings. He slides his hand down to my ass.

"Well, I guess in a way, that's kinda perfect. Now everyone is paired up evenly. It would've been weird with her being the only person without a date." I hump my shoulders at his words.

"Yeah, I guess." Danny massages my ass slowly while we sit there in silence. My hormones should be jumping all over the place right now, but him bringing up Pam took me out of the mood. I feel so awful for being out here partying without her, especially since this is the one group of guys that she's overly fascinated with. I feel like I'm stabbing her in the back, even though I'm not completely sure how.

"You good?" Danny wonders, breaking up my thoughts about Pam. I grin while shaking my head, yes. "You sure? You seemed kind of spaced out for a minute." I look at Danny seriously, wondering if I can trust him with my personal thoughts. He looks at me attentively as if I can. I sigh before deciding to lay a few things out in the open.

"Pam has a major crush on Dame; she has since high school. She really, really likes him so what happened earlier today with him and Tanisha really hurt her feelings. Now, I just feel bad for her, I guess." Danny nods his head as if he understands where I'm coming from but he doesn't say anything. I turn to look at Richie and Shay playfully splashing each other in the pool, "I don't know. I know it's probably no big deal to you because you're probably used to women having crushes on y'all, I just don't like seeing her in pain."

"It's not that it's no big deal to me, it's just that…" Danny gets quiet as if he's trying to choose his words wisely, "Dame is my brother and I love him, but he's a douchebag. Period. There's no way to get around saying it. He's completely unable to be with one chick at a time. Of course females have crushes on him, and he never turns down any of them, either. He'll fuck every last one of them if they let him. Pam is too nice of a girl to be wrapped up in a guy like my brother. I'ma be honest with you, he doesn't deserve a woman like her."

I make a shocked face at his revelation as we make eye contact. I can tell that he didn't want to say those things about his brother but he felt it was necessary that I knew. I smile at him for opening up to me a little more. He flashes his perfect smile back.

"How about we get in the pool? I'm tired of Richie and Shay having all the fun," I exclaim while standing up from his lap. He grabs me from behind and pulls my body between his legs. He kisses my left ass cheek through my swimsuit and I jump with surprise. I look down at him.

"Sorry, I just couldn't help myself." I giggle and he kisses it again, "I know I said I wanted hugs whenever we saw each other, but now I think I want kisses instead. Don't be alarmed by my lips whenever they touch you. I'm liable to kiss whatever body part you put in front of my face." My eyes get big with interest. I smirk before slowly turning my body around. He smiles devilishly once he's face-to-face with my pussy.

"Wow," He exclaims, staring at my fat monkey through my black swim bottoms. He leans in and lays his lips against her. "Can I kiss it with nothing covering it?" He looks up at me sexily. My body gets warm with excitement from his request. I blush without answering. He seductively stands to his feet and my anxiety grows once his strong body presses against mine. He grabs my ass and mushes our crotches together.

"I think it's time for you to give me a tour of your room." He speaks to me in a stern, sexual tone. My anxiety climbs even higher. I really like Danny, but I just met him. *Is it a good idea to let him in my bed so soon?*

"Come on. I promise, won't nothing happen that you don't want to happen. I just want to kiss her… please?" He flashes that award-winning smile again and I smack my lips. He knows damn well that he's not going to give me some head without expecting something in return. He reads the look on my face, "What? You don't believe me?"

"Danny, come on. Your fine ass wants to go up to my room just to put your head between my thighs and that's it? Yes, I definitely find that hard to believe." His face goes from sexy to serious.

"I think what you're trying to say is that I look too good to be begging to eat pussy-"

"No! I didn't mean it like that-"

"Let me finish, because I think we have some crossed wires here." He sounds offended so I try to give him some space but he doesn't let me go, "No, I don't have to beg to eat pussy to get ass, but that's not what our relationship is about, at least that's what I thought. I like you, Amber. You're different from all of the other broads around here. It's just something about you that makes me so comfortable, like I can be myself around you. You're down to Earth, easy to talk to, and you're absolutely gorgeous. I think with that combination, you deserved to feel good... to be pleased. That's all this is about, really. I want you to know that I'll do anything to make you feel good, whether that's mentally, emotionally, or physically. And you did just put your pussy in my face after I said I'm liable to kiss whatever you put there, so I thought that was your way of telling me that-"

"Come on." I grab him by the hand and drag him towards the house's back door. He stops in his tracks and I turn around to face him.

"Wait a minute. So now you want to go up to your room?" He still has an aggravated look on his face and I smile. I walk up to him and kiss his lips for the first time.

"Yes I do. Is that a problem?" He sighs loudly before shaking his head, no.

"Good, and please be quiet. I don't want us waking up the whole household."

CHAPTER EIGHT

Danny wastes no time snatching my bikini bottoms off and spreading my legs wide on the bed. *"I'm so glad I shaved,"* is all I keep thinking as he carefully spreads my pussy lips with his fingers.

"She's beautiful," he whispers before kissing my clit softly. My body jerks at the feeling of his warm breath traveling down my vaginal crack.

It's been forever since I've been intimate with a man, but I'm going to try my best to keep it together tonight.

"Mmm…" He moans after getting his first real taste of my delectable flavor. His tongue comes out to play for a second but then his lips take over again. "How do you like to be eaten?" He pauses to ask me. He glances up at me from down below and I bite my bottom lip.

"Just like that," I answer in a satisfied tone. He looks at my pussy again before placing his lips back around my clit.

"Mmm…" He moans again after my warm juices begin to flow down his throat. I can tell he's no stranger to orally pleasing a woman. I reach for my pillow and grab it. He's going to make me cum if he keeps this up.

"Fuck!" I curse with my face smashed against the pillow. He flat tongues my entire vagina, starting at my dripping entrance and stopping at my rock hard clitoris. He flicks at it with the tip of his wet tongue. My body trembles with the same rhythm. His lips take over again and he slurps up my secretions as they leak from my contracting opening. He sucks on my clit passionately. I lose my damn mind.

"Yes!" I shout in the pillow loudly. I grab the back of his fade. I hold his head in place to let him know he's right where he needs to be. He reaches around my thigh and uses his hand to lift my clitoral hood, exposing my clit to his lips' suction even more.

"I'm cumming!" I announce right before my body begins spasming. He keeps his mouth wrapped around my spot no matter how violently I shake. I try my best not to scream at the top of my lungs.

I don't think I've ever cum this hard in my life!

He finally has mercy on me and frees my clit from his lips' grasp, "Mmm, you taste good, baby," he whispers after sitting up in my bed. He uses the back of his hand to wipe my juices from around his mouth. I lay there breathing hard, still trying to regain my composure. He stares at me as if he's studying my body's curves. I place the pillow on top of me shyly.

"Why'd you do that?" He asks, sounding slightly disappointed that I fucked up his visual. I shrug embarrassingly.

"I don't know, just a little self-conscious, I guess." He snatches the pillow off of me and lays on top of my half naked body. He stares into my eyes.

"What do you have to be self-conscious about? I told you, you're absolutely gorgeous." I blush at how sure he sounds and he glances down at my lips. He leans in and kisses me deeply. We fall into a makeout moment that lasts longer than it was intended to last. Our lips are tangled up so passionately that we begin to sweat.

"Mmm, baby, we should slow down," Danny moans in a low tone. I stare at his sweaty face with disappointment.

"But I don't want to." He takes a deep breath.

"Baby, we have to. I only carry condoms in my wallet, and I left my wallet in my jean pocket at home. If we keep this up, I'm going to want to be inside of you." I make a dispirited face. He displays a similar expression. We lay there in silence, staring at each other as if we're waiting for the other person to say what we both seem to be thinking.

Danny hesitates, "I mean, I am safe. I haven't had unprotected sex in years, but I still get tested every six months." I listen to his confession and take a deep breath.

"Well, I've only had unprotected sex once, but I was so terrified of getting pregnant that I never did it again." Danny's face loses all hope as he tries to climb off of me. I stop him before he does, "But, this will only be a one time thing. Like, you'll be prepared next time, right?" Danny nods his head yes quickly.

"Of course." He leans down and kisses me again. "Are you sure about this?" He stares at me seriously and I gesture that I'm OK with it. He sits up on his knees to untie his swim trunks.

"Just make sure you pull out in time." He slides off his bottoms and tosses them to the floor.

"I promise."

***

Danny plunges his thick dick in and out of me with deep, long strokes. I hold on to his back for dear life, trying my best not to shout out loud in extreme pleasure. My eyes roll as he places his forehead on mine. Every time he speeds up, he wraps his mouth around my lips to stop me from screaming.

"Like that?" He grunts out while hitting me with small, hard thrusts. My legs spread wider to let him in further. They shake violently with pleasure.

"Danny! Yes!" He places one of my legs on his shoulder and grabs my ass with his hand. He pounds at my swollen pussy. I reach for my pillow again.

"Fuck that pillow," he spits out before placing his mouth over mine again. He strokes me faster, causing me to cum instantly.

"MMM!" I moan loudly between his lips. He doesn't break his pace, making me cum nonstop for what seems like forever. He pounds at me before his kisses become broken.

"Shit, baby! Shit… I'm about to cum!" He slides in and out of me a few more times before pulling his dick out and cumming all over my thigh. He fights the urge to moan out loud while his sperm erupts from his penishead. He collapses on the side of me shortly thereafter. We both breath hard with bliss.

"Wow...that was... amazing," Danny mumbles between breaths. I nod my head as if I agree.

"Yes, it most definitely was, especially since I haven't had sex in almost a year." Danny looks over at me with a stunned expression.

"You haven't had sex in a year? Are you serious?" I look away from him embarrassingly.

"Yeah. Very." He rolls his body towards me and lays on his arm.

"Well, why not?" I sigh at the thought of my ex-boyfriend, Dwayne. I've tried my best not to talk about him, especially since we had such a painful break-up.

"To be completely honest with you, I don't really believe in having sex with someone if I'm not in a relationship with them, so the reason why I haven't had sex in a year is because that's how long I've been single." Danny stares at me admirably. He leans over and kisses my lips sweetly.

"Wow, I don't think I've ever heard anyone say that before. That's so fucking dope of you." He grabs me and pulls me closer to him. I lay on his chest, listening to his heartbeat in its natural rhythm. The sound soothes me and I close my eyes. Danny rubs my hair gently.

"Well, I guess that means that we're in a relationship, then."

"Hmm?" I ask softly, barely hearing anything he's saying. The sandman is calling my name...
I'm drifting away to sleepland…

"Amber! Amber, wake up!" I open my eyes suddenly to the sound of Pam's voice. She hurries over to my bed and shakes me.

"Amber!" I raise off of Danny's chest and look at her. Danny rubs the sleep from his eyes after her hysterical tone wakes him up, too.

"Pam, what is it?" I ask irritably in a groggy voice. I squint my eyes after seeing the sun shining through my window.

"You have to get Danny out of here now! Ma just woke up! He has to go!" I jump up quickly after comprehending her words, searching for my bikini bottoms expeditiously. I toss Danny his trunks and he hurriedly slides them on underneath the cover. "Hurry up! I'll stall her!" Pam rushes out of my room and closes the door. Danny jumps up quickly and slides on his Nike's.

"Dammit! My bad, baby. I didn't mean to fall asleep. Everything about last night was just so perfect-"

"Agreed," I say quickly while opening my blue curtains. I look at the piece of roof outside of my window and then the 20-foot drop underneath it. I sigh with defeat after realizing that him leaving out that way isn't an option. He joins me at the window and looks out of it as well. We stand there in silence for a few seconds.

"I can make it." I look at him like he's crazy.

"No the hell you can't... are you insane?" He smiles as if I just challenged him.

"A little." He slides my window open and I grab his arm.

"Seriously, Danny. This is crazy. You can just leave out of the front door. My mom will be a little shocked that you stayed here all night, but I'm grown and she's just going to have to deal with it-"

"Baby, listen. I really don't want our relationship starting off like this. If your mom finds out that I spent the night, she fa sho' won't like me, and I can't have that. Moms are supposed to love me!" I shake my head humorously at him before chuckling at his small rant. He sticks one leg out of the window and I grab his arm again.

"Wait a minute, our relationship? What relationship?" He looks at me as if I just asked him a stupid question.

"The one we're in…" He says slowly as if I should know already. I turn red with surprise. I blush at him.

"Oh wow… OK. I- I didn't know that." He sticks his leg back in the window and faces me.

"You told me last night that you only have sex when you're in a relationship, and I can't have you breaking your personal standards for me. So, if you only give yourself to guys that you're dating exclusively, then we're dating exclusively now, OK?" He nods his head yes slowly as if he wants me to agree with him. I smile at him and nod my head yes as well.

"Good. See, that's exactly what I thought." He kisses me quickly before climbing out of the window. He hurries to the edge of the roof and slides off of it like the height is no big deal to him. My heart beats swiftly at the thought of him hurting himself, but I see him jogging along the side of the house shortly thereafter. I smile in amazement.

He must be a superhero or some shit.

"Doll, are you OK? I knocked but you never answered." I turn around suddenly when I hear my mom's voice coming from behind me. She takes a few steps inside of my room with a concerned look on her face. Pam rushes in behind her, looking around my room nervously. She looks relieved once she notices that Danny is no longer in sight.

"I'm sorry, ma. I must not have heard you. I'm actually just waking up." My mom listens to my explanation while staring curiously at my attire.

"Must've been one hell of a night for you to still be wearing your swimsuit." I look down at my body, completely forgetting about what I was wearing. I notice Danny's dried nut on my leg and lay my hand over it speedily. I think of a lie to tell her quickly.

"Yeah, I think I had a little too much to drink last night. I just came in here and dove right in bed. I wasn't even thinking about changing." I giggle nervously. My mom stares at me strangely.

"Yeah… OK… well, I'm about to start breakfast for everyone. It's a lot of y'all, so I wanted to get started early."

"I can help," Pam offers and my mom smiles at her.

"Thanks, but no need. I'm just glad to finally have something to do around here." My mother turns around and walks out of my room. Pam walks towards the exit as well.

"Pam?" I say before she leaves out of the door. She turns around to face me.

"Thanks for the heads up. That was really good looking out." She grins at me before attempting to leave again, "But, I do have one question, though. How did you know that I had Danny in here?" She looks out into the hallway to make sure that no one is around before answering my question.

"Girl, your bed was loud... like, extremely loud. I have no idea how you two didn't wake up mom and dad!" I cover my mouth embarrassingly.
Shit! I had no idea!

"I didn't hear much moaning, but I heard that headboard nonstop. At first I thought it was y'all outside in the pool but then the constant rhythm of the beating told me exactly what it was." I giggle and she shakes her head.

"Fuck! I'm so sorry if we kept you up, Pam. That is so embarrassing." She shakes her head with a smile.

"Don't be embarrassed, I'm sure I would've done the same thing if the opportunity presented itself." We both laugh and she walks towards the door.

"Pam, you were right, too." She turns around and gives me a questioning look.

"About what?"

"That saying. It's definitely true. Devul dick comes straight from Lucifer himself."

CHAPTER NINE

I walk around this town's version of a mall and sigh at the shopping options. This place only has about 15 stores, most of which I would never shop in. I walk next to Pam as we watch Tanisha, Rochelle, and Shay window shop. Shay frowns her face up for the 10th time.

"Ugh, not one piece of plus-size clothing in this damn place! What, fat bitches don't live here or something?" Pam and I giggle at her outburst.

"I'm telling you, this place is wack. Even though I can fit most of this shit, I'd never wear any of it! Like this for example, look at this hideous shit! Who would wear something like this?" Rochelle points to a tri-colored pants suit that's being displayed on one of the mannequins in a boutique window. Pam makes an offended face.

"Me. I have that outfit." We all roar with laughter and Pam folds her arms, "Hey! We don't have much to choose from around here! We gotta wear what we can find." We wrap up our laughter and continue walking.

"Why don't you ever go into the city, Pam? You are literally like an hour away from Atlanta." Shay asks, staring inside of another store's window. Pam humps her shoulders.

"I've always wanted to, but I guess I never really had anyone to go with."

"What about your friends? Why not go with them?" Shay continues to pry. She stares at Pam while waiting for a reply.

"To be honest, all of my friends left after graduation. They all went to colleges in different states. I wanted to go away to college, too, but I decided to stay behind to take care of my dad instead. Of course, that was before he met Amber's mom."

"Amber, how did your mom meet her dad anyway?" Rochelle inquires, joining in on the conversation. We continue to walk slowly in the nearly empty establishment.

"My Aunt Christine lives in Atlanta and ma came down here to visit her one day. Apparently, Aunt Christine was looking for a car, so her and ma went to one of Craig's dealerships. He happened to be up there that day, so my aunt got a good deal on a ride and my mom found the love of her life. The rest is history."

"Aww…" Tanisha blurts out in a sarcastic tone. I roll my eyes at her.

"Damn! I forgot all about Aunt Christine! I keep forgetting that your Uncle Chris is no longer a man," Shay exclaims. Pam's eyes get big.

"Wait a minute! What?" I snicker at her reaction.

"Yeah. My uncle moved down to Atlanta to finalize his transition from a man to a woman. He's always lived as a woman anyway, now he just has the parts to match."

"That's crazy," Pam admits while shaking her head. I hump my shoulders.

"I mean, as long as he's happy, I'm all for it."

"Shit! I just got a brilliant ass idea!" Tanisha stops suddenly to blurt out. She turns around to face all of us.

"How about we go into the city tonight? Take Pam on her first big city adventure?" Tanisha grins really wide and everyone looks at each other. I look at Pam who's not sure what to say.

"I mean, I'm down if she is," I add, knocking my body playfully into hers. She looks at me with unsure eyes. I give her a warm smile.

"Come on! It'll be fun! Let's show you how city girls do it!" Tanisha starts twerking randomly with her small, spandex shorts on and we all giggle at her ratchetness. She drops it low a couple of times before acknowledging us again.

"I mean, it sounds like it could be fun. OK… I'll go." We all start cheering happily. Pam gets excited, too. *I'm glad my friends are finally opening up to her.*

"Just don't wear that damn pants suit," Rochelle teases, pointing back at the window she saw it in. "I'll let you borrow something before you put that shit on." Pam smacks her lips and we all laugh.

"Don't worry about it, Pam. Between the four of us, I'm sure we'll find something for her to wear," I comment, looping my arm into hers.

"How about we invite the fellas along?" Tanisha says randomly, staring at all of us with a mischievous look in her eyes.

"Why? We spent all yesterday with them! Can't we go and meet some new guys?" Rochelle whines out. Shay looks at her crazily.

"Meet new guys? In Atlanta? Where everyone is on the down-low?" Shay shakes her head quickly, "No thank you." Rochelle nods her head as if she has a point. She sighs with defeat.

"Why? What's wrong with Bruno? Brotha is fine." Tanisha admits. We all shake our heads in unison. *Bruno does have that sexy thug appeal thing going on.*

"It's not that he's not fine, because brotha is most definitely that, it's just that… well… he scares the shit out of me." We all make shocked expressions.

"Come again?" I ask immediately. She looks down embarrassingly.

"I mean… we were talking last night and everything, finally getting to know each other better, and then the drinks started kicking in and the sexual tension started building up, so we decided to get in the pool and feel each other up a little bit. Well, things were going well when he was touching on me; I mean, he made me cum and everything… but girrrl, when I touched him…" She makes a frightened face. We all stare at her, impatiently waiting for her to finish. She swallows the lump growing in her throat, "That man has an Anaconda snake in his damn drawers and I don't want no parts of it!" The other girls and I erupt with laughter. Rochelle makes a face as if she's serious, making us laugh even harder.

"Girl, bye! You trippin'! That sounds like a perfect reason to see that man again!" Tanisha exclaims. We all nod in agreement again. Rochelle shakes her head no as if she's not interested.

"Nish, I don't know, man. That motherfucka was huge! Like, where are you planning on putting that thang, sir? No, no no… not down there." She grabs her crotch and shakes her head no again. We all laugh once more.

"I don't know, Chelle. You should try it, you might like it," I suggest with a huge smile on my face. She looks at me and smacks her lips.

"Mmhmm… you would say that after disappearing all night with Mr. Daniel Devul." I make a guilty face as everyone in the group stares at me.

"Yeah, especially after talking shit about me for wanting to get it in with Dame." Tanisha adds her two cents and I narrow my eyes at her.
Of course she would bring that up.

"Listen, he just wanted a tour of my room, that's it," I say while trying to keep a straight face. Everyone smacks their lips at me.

"Ohhh...OK. So did he have to pay extra for the tour of your vagina, or was that included in the package?" I cut my eyes at Rochelle after everyone snickers. I fold my arms defensively.

"It wasn't even like that! I mean… it was supposed to just be him giving me some head, but then-" I become tongue-tied while trying to explain myself. Everyone shakes their heads at me but Pam and Shay.

"Girl, fuck what they're talking about. I'm just glad you finally got you some, shit," Shay states, looping her arm through mine, "Because after what happened with Dwayne, I thought your ass would never get that close to a man again." Tanisha and Rochelle both quickly remember my ordeal with my ex and their faces soften up. They both walk over to me as well.

"Yeah, my bad. I didn't mean anything by what I said. I was just fucking with you," Tanisha aplogizes. I smile at her.

"It's no biggie… and I'm sorry for giving you a hard time about Dame. You're a grown ass woman. You have the right to do what you want." She makes an uneasy face.

"I probably should've listened to y'all, honestly. He only seems to care about his own pleasure and not mine. I have yet to get anything from him besides a mouth full of sperm. I'm going to tell him tonight that it's my turn to cum, dammit," she tries to say with a straight face, but we can all tell she's somewhat embarrassed by her words. We're speechless to say the least. She smiles awkwardly before we all continue walking again.

"Thank God Richie is nothing like that. He's so tough, but sweet, just like hard candy or some shit." Shay grins at the thought of her new male interest, "And he's so fucking strong and manly. All night, I just kept hoping that he'd ask to take me to his place so that I could wear him out! That man is so fine…" she lets out a lustful sigh. "When I see him again, it's going down, and I'm being so serious right now-"

"We can tell," Rochelle interrupts. Shay smacks her lips at her.

"Anyway, let's get the fuck out of here. I have better shit than this in my suitcase," Tanisha announces as if she's heard enough. "We need time to get ready anyway because we're going to Atlanta tonight!"

CHAPTER TEN

"Don't you ladies look hot!" Ma says with an amazed look on her face. We all glance in her direction and smile, "And Pam, I'm so happy you're getting out tonight! Make sure you have a good time." Pam assures my mom that she will before kissing her on the cheek. My mother leaves my room and closes the door.

"Girls, do y'all think I'm doing too much with this dress on?" Tanisha stares at herself in my full-length mirror while she waits for us to reply. We all look at each other like she knows damn well she is.

"Nisha, when ain't you doing too much?" Shay asks, staring at the sheer purple mini-dress Tanisha has on with the matching bra and panty set underneath.

"That's a dress? Oh, I thought that was lingerie," Pam teases and we all make amusing instigating noises. Tanisha turns around and gives her a scolding look.

"Oh, I see sis got jokes tonight." Pam smiles innocently.

"Anyway, what time are the guys going to be here?" Rochelle asks the room. She stares in the vanity mirror while applying her dark eyeshadow.

"Danny said around eight or so."

"Oh, OK. So, are we following them, or they're following us, or what?" Shay questions, fixing the bottom of her flowy, black blouse. She paired it with matching leggings and some cute, glittery flats.

"Actually, they're picking us up. Richie has a Suburban that's big enough to fit us all." All of the women look pleasantly surprised, especially Shay.

"Excuse me," Pam says suddenly before getting up from my bed and walking out of my room. The girls watch her leave, but they don't think twice about it. I, on the other hand, start to worry about her. I decide to check on her after I finish getting ready. I knock at her door before cracking it slightly.

"Pam, can I come in?"

"Sure," she answers while sitting in her desk chair. She spins around to look at me when I step inside of her room.

"Hey. I just wanted to make sure you were OK." She makes a distraught face. I take a deep breath, "What's the matter?"

"Well, I guess I was OK with going as long as I wasn't forced to be around Dame and Tanisha, but now I have to sit in Richie's truck with them for a whole hour while they do God knows what right next to me. I just- I don't think I can stomach it."

I sigh before heading over to her bed to sit down, "I'm sorry, Pam. If I would've known this was going to bother you, I never would've told him that we'd ride with them."

"It's OK. I'm a fool for getting so bent out of shape over a man that's never really liked me anyway. I mean, what the fuck is wrong with me?" She shakes her head with shame, "The only real relationship I had was with my married teacher who I'm sure was just taking advantage of me because I was young and impressionable, and how could I even consider that to be real, anyway? That shit was nowhere near real, but it was still more real than anything else I've ever had with any other guy in my life." She becomes disgusted at the realization, "Wow, how pathetic is that?" Pam feels sorry for herself. I stand to my feet and walk over to her.

"Pam, you are being so unnecessarily hard on yourself. First of all, fuck Mr. Stanson with his creepy, pedophilic ass! He didn't deserve you, he deserved jail time… and fuck Damien and his promiscious ass dick. He doesn't deserve you either, and that came straight from Danny's mouth. You deserve a man that's going to treat you like a queen and make you feel as beautiful as you are." She grins at my words, "And hopefully, you getting out tonight will show you that it's a whole world out there full of men that's better looking and more deserving of you than these fools around here are."

Pam stands to her feet after my overly emotional rant as if what I said suddenly motivated her. She smiles at me before giving me a hug, "Thank you so much for saying those things, Amber. That was exactly what I needed to hear."

I smile back at her, "I only said those things because they're true." I look her up and down quickly, "Now, how about I help you finish getting ready? I can do your makeup for you, help you pick out some shoes to go with that dress that Rochelle let you borrow, and then put your braids up into a cute bun or something." She nods her head yes happily, "And I promise, you'll definitely be turning heads tonight."

***

Richie pulls up in a brand-new, all black Suburban that quickly impresses the shit out of us. It's 24 inch rims roll to a stop and my stomach starts to hurt at the thought of seeing Danny again. All four of the men eventually hop out of the truck, walking in their usual, attention-grabbing way. Danny has on a striped, tri-blue button-up with navy blue slacks and matching shoes. His clothes fit him in all of the right places, causing my pussy to drip uncontrollably like a leaky faucet.

I hope he remembered the condoms this time.

Richie is wearing an all black, tight V-neck tee and black, slim-fitting jeans with black casual boots. As simple as he's dressed however, he still looks damn good in his clothes.

Richie can wear a damn potato sack and still be the man. His attire matches Shay's and I instantly smile at the coincidence.

Bruno and Dame are both dressed similarly, sporting name brand tees, blue jeans, Jordan gym shoes, and huge chains around their necks. Bruno's fitted hat is pulled down so far on his head that you can barely see his eyes. He walks with a heavy stride, making what Rochelle said about him make sense.

He has to be carrying a huge load between his legs!

Dame's fitted is on his head backwards as if he's not interested in hiding his handsome face. Even though I can't stand his personality, I must admit…

Dame is one beautiful ass Devul.

"Ladies, ready to go?" Richie asks in that irresistible voice of his. He sticks his hand out for Shay and she grabs it with a smile. Danny reaches for me and pulls me into him. He kisses me so passionately that everyone stops to stare at us. My clit begins thumping with the rhythm of my pounding heartbeat. We separate before things get out of control like they did last night.

"Damn," Tanisha mumbles after me and Danny's lips finally unravel.

"Damn is right," Danny says sexily before taking me under his arm.

"You alright?" Bruno asks Rochelle curiously. I look over at her and see the nervous expression on her face. She makes eye contact with me and I mouth for her to relax. She finally nods her head, yes, to his question and puts her hand in his.

Wow, she really is afraid of that man's penis!

"What's up, Pam?" Dame says, bringing up the rear. Pam looks shocked by his random acknowledgement of her. Tanisha looks at Dame angrily and puts her hands on her hips.

"Damn, really? You're just gonna speak to her before even speaking to me?" Dame makes an uninterested face at Tanisha.

"Girl, chill out. I just saw you last night but I didn't see Pam. That's my homegirl." Tanisha folds her arms with a smack of her lips and stomps towards Richie's truck. She climbs in the front passenger side after Richie and Shay both get in on the front driver's side. Dame ignores her attitude completely and smiles at Pam.

"What happened to you last night? I was looking forward to kicking it with you like old times. We ain't chopped it up in a while." Pam blushes hard while looking down at her small clutch purse. She humps her shoulders shyly.

"I was a little tired and decided to turn in early." Dame takes a step towards her and grabs her hand.

"Well, how about you hang with me tonight?" Pam blushes harder.

"OK... That- that sounds good." They walk past Danny and I, "And by the way, you're looking really good tonight." She giggles at his compliment and I smack my lips. I look over at Danny and he shakes his head.

"Dame will be Dame." I sigh at his statement. We start walking towards the car as well.

"I know, and that's what I'm afraid of."

CHAPTER ELEVEN

The girls and I laugh hysterically at the Devuls as they attempt to recap the events of their last time driving to Atlanta. They argue with each other nonstop because one brother will remember an incident happening totally differently than another brother. The main two guys with the biggest disagreements are Bruno and Dame. They are fussing at each other so much that it almost seems like they're about to fight.

"Man, y'all chill out! Don't nobody wanna hear that shit!" Richie's voice thunders out and the whole truck gets quiet. He looks over at Shay and shakes his head, "I'm sorry for yelling in your ear, beautiful, but these motherfuckas get on my nerves sometimes." Danny snickers at Richie's outburst.

He leans his body into mine, "I'm telling you, when we were kids, Richie was the only person that could get Bruno and Dame to listen. When they got in trouble at school, they never called momma, they'd just find Richie."

"Man, shut up," Bruno spits out and we both look over at him. I'm sandwiched in between the two men, making it easy for him to hear everything that Danny's saying about him. Bruno makes a stone serious face and I slide closer to Danny.

Rochelle is right, Bruno is scary as hell.

I glance back at Rochelle in the third row sitting next to Pam and Dame. She stares out of the small, back window as if something is on her mind. She looks like she's having an awful time and I feel bad for her.

Dame is whispering in Pam's ear, making her giggle nonstop. I try to catch eye contact with her, but Dame is the only person she's paying attention to at the moment. I sigh with worry.

I'll kick Dame's ass if he hurts her again.

I look up front at Tanisha and watch her take filtered selfies for a few minutes. She recruits Shay for a couple of them, posting several of the photos to her social media pages. Even though Dame just curved the shit out of her, she still seems to be in good spirits. That's one of the advantages of being loose, I guess.

There's no need to chase em' when you can easily replace em'.

Atlanta's city lights start coming into view and everyone stares out of the windows. Richie turns down the J. Cole playing from the speakers, "So, what should we get into tonight?" No one answers right away and Richie gets irritated, "Come on, I know I didn't drive all the way here for nothing."

"Actually Richie, the point of tonight was to show Pam the city since she's never seen it." I put my stepsister on blast and she makes an embarrassed face.

"What? You've never been to the 'A'?" Dame asks surprisedly. She shakes her head no. "Don't worry, I'll make sure you have a great time." Dame licks his lips, prompting Pam to blush all over again. I roll my eyes at his audacity.

His pussy hopping is so disrespectful.

"Richie, let's go to the club or something. I need to find someone new to play with," Tanisha blurts out as a clapback to Dame's blatant shift of interest. He snickers as if he knows what she's trying to do, but doesn't care.

"Is that cool with everybody?" Richie shouts out and everyone agrees that it is. "Alright, then. I know just the spot."

***

Richie stops at a bar that has a two-dollar Tuesday banner outside of it. He pulls up in the valet parking lane and everyone jumps out once the valet driver appears.

"Scratch it and that's yo' ass," he growls to the guy before giving him the truck's keys. The young man swallows hard before getting inside of the Suburban and closing the door.

Shay wraps her arm around Richie's, "That wasn't very nice." He looks at her cute face and smiles, "You're right, gorgeous. That wasn't. I'll apologize to him with a nice ass tip."

We walk inside the bar and look shocked at how many people are in attendance. The only uninhabited space is a huge VIP booth with a blue rope around it.

"Excuse me… miss!" Richie shouts in an attempt to get a waitress's attention. The bass in his voice carries better than the bass in the music. The random women standing near us all turn to look at him. Shay holds on to him tightly, sending a message to the other ladies that he's taken for tonight. The waitress eventually walks over to see what he wants, "I was wondering, who's booth is that?"

"No one's tonight. It's mostly occupied on the weekends."

"OK, so how do we get it?" She leans in while she talks.

"Well, you have to give me $250, and then it's all yours." The girls and I look at each other like this bitch has lost her mind.

$250 for a booth?! That's absurd!

Bruno steps up immediately with a fistful of money. He counts out $500 and hands it to the lady.

"Aye, and I need three bottles of vodka and some chicken wings." The girls and I look at each other again, this time with impressed looks on our faces.

I walk over to Rochelle, "Oh, Bruno's showing out tonight!" She laughs at my comment.

"I see! He may just get a little bit of this lovin' after all."

The men walk over to the VIP section and move the giant rope. Bruno helps us step up on the red carpeted space one by one. The men step up right after us. We take a look at the big, black U-shaped velvet couch but no one sits on it. We turn around to face the fellas.

"Thank you, Bruno. This was really nice of you." Rochelle flirts with him and he licks his lips. "The pleasure is all mine." She smiles at him sexily.

"And thanks to you, too, Richie. We appreciate you driving us all this way just to show us a good time." Shay smiles at Richie with a smitten glare and Richie grabs her gently around the waist.

"Dance with me?" He steps down from the VIP stage before she gets a chance to answer. He helps her down and they disappear onto the crowded dance floor.

"Dancing doesn't sound like a bad idea. Care to show me what you got?" Rochelle propositions Bruno. He nods his head, yes, while taking her hand in his.

"Baby, how about you? Wanna dance?" I look at Danny's handsome face.

"Actually, I was hoping to have a drink first. My dancing ain't the best so I need a little liquor courage to get me on the dance floor." He grins.

"Ok, no problem. I'll grab us something from the bar."

"But Bruno just ordered all of those bottles," I remind Danny. He humps his shoulders as if he doesn't care.

"That was his money. I'm going to buy my lady a drink," he broadcasts with his chest poked out.

"Pam, I'll grab us something, too," Dame adds. They hop off the tall step together and make their way towards the other side of the club. Tanisha glances at Dame's back and rolls her eyes at him.

"A drink doesn't sound half bad right about now." She signals for a random guy to help her down from the VIP section and several come to her rescue. She flirts with them all as soon as her feet touch the floor. She starts sweet-talking them out of their coins while they slowly move towards the bar. Pam shakes her head disgustingly at her antics.

I move closer to her, "So, are you having a good time?" A huge smile appears on her face.

"The best." I look at her with a worried expression. She smacks her lips as if she already knows what I'm thinking, "I know what you're going to say, and I can't say that I don't agree with you, but please Amber, let me just enjoy my night."

"But Dame is a scumbag, though-"

"I just said I know! But I really like him-"

"He was literally just kissing on Tanisha less than 24 hours ago! He has no respect for women-"

"No, he has no respect for her! But how could he when she doesn't even respect herself?" We both get quiet after realizing that we're traveling down a road that neither one of us wants to be on. I smile caringly at her.

"Look… Pam, I don't want to argue about this, and I don't want it to seem like I'm trying to tell you what to do, but I just want you to be careful, that's all. You see how Dame is. I've only known him for a couple of days-"

"That's right, *you've* only known him for a couple of days but *I've* known him a lot longer than that! This literally has nothing to do with you because he and I were friends before you even existed to me. You can't pass moral judgements, anyway. You knew Danny two days before fucking him raw. You think I didn't see the dried up cum on your leg?" She blows up at me, causing me to take an appalling step back. I put my hands up peacefully.

"I apologize if I've offended you, and I promise, I won't butt in again."

CHAPTER TWELVE

Pam and I keep our distance as the bottles of vodka go from three, to two, to one. Even though I've had my share of shots, I still didn't have as much as everyone else did. Even Pam drank a nice amount of liquor and she doesn't even drink.

I see Dame is rubbing off on her in a bad way already.

Things are getting really hot and heavy between Richie and Shay. They are making out so loud that the music can barely drown them out. They've been going at it for 10 minutes straight without coming up for air once. Dame and Bruno both snicker in amazement.

"Damn, I don't think I've ever seen Richie this into a chick before," Dame confesses to the group. Richie and Shay are so wrapped up in each other that they can't hear what's being said about them. Bruno nods his head in agreement before leaning back on the couch. He fixes his hat and Rochelle glances over at him.

"You good?" He asks her. She makes a face as if she's buzzed out of her mind.

"Do you know that I was so afraid of the size of your dick that I stopped liking you?" Everyone's eyes get big around the couch and Dame laughs hysterically. Bruno gawks at her with a strange look on his face.

"What?"

"Your dick. It is so big that it made me want to clinch my ass cheeks together and run for the hills." I laugh out loud this time. Danny balls his face up at the topic of conversation before excusing himself to the bathroom.

"I ain't gonna lie, Bruno. When she told us that, the first thing I thought was 'I gotta see this motherfucka'," Tanisha slurs out. She looks down at his crotch and then back in his eyes. Bruno grins with flattery.

"Bro, you heard her. Show her your dick," Dame suggests stupidly. I smack my lips at his ignorant ass idea.

"Fool, shut up. What do I look like pulling my dick out in front of all these people?" Dame looks around at the people in the bar.

"Ain't nobody paying attention to us. Look, I'll stand up in front of you so that can't nobody else see. Give the ladies what they want and show 'em your cock." Dame stands to his feet amusingly and puts his back towards us. Tanisha slides closer to Bruno and both her and Rochelle stare down at his zipper. He looks at both of the ladies in disbelief.

"Y'all really want me to pull my dick out right here, right now?"

"Yes!" Tanisha and Rochelle say in unison. Pam and I decide not to engage. We try our best to look away, but our eyes keep finding their way back to Bruno's jeans.

"Alright…" Bruno unfastens his belt and unbuttons his pants. He pulls down his zipper in a suspenseful way. He digs inside of his flannel boxers carefully and lifts his body up some as if he's sitting on his penis. My mouth falls open with skepticism.

His meat can't possibly be that large!

He grabs the base of it with his hand. He shimmies it from the boxer's hole and it falls on top of his jeans like a giant pepperoni log.

"Gotdamn!" Tanisha shouts out, reaching over to grab it. Rochelle pops her hand quickly.

"Hey! I said you could see it, not touch it!" Tanisha smacks her lips disappointedly. Pam's eyes get big once she spots it and she looks away with a wowed expression on her face. I stare at it harder than I should, allowing my mouth to water at the thought of putting the huge schlong in my mouth.

"Damn, Bruno… and it's not even hard," Rochelle points out, deciding to stroke it around it's head. It grows upright and he stops her.

"That's enough." She grins devilishly.

"Can we continue this later?" He smirks back at her.

"Damn Chelle, you're so lucky. Bruno's dick makes Dame's look childish." Bruno tucks his meat away quickly before laughing at what Tanisha said. Dame turns around with a chuckle.

"It was big enough to fit in your mouth… twice." She frowns up at him and he smirks at her. She gets up and bumps past him, nearly falling off the stage. He catches her and pulls her back up, "I should've let your drunk ass fall." She snatches away from him and carefully eases her way out of VIP. She stumbles over to a table full of men and sits on one of their laps.

"Hoe," Dame mumbles under his breath while watching her fraternizing with strangers. I cut my eyes at him.

"Dame, you have no room to call anyone a hoe." He looks at me with a weird expression on his face.

"I call em' like I see em'." I give him a repulsing look.

"You weren't saying that about her yesterday when you had your tongue stuffed down her throat," Rochelle jumps in with a defensive tone. Dame laughs obnoxiously.

"Actually, I did. I knew she was a hoe from the first time I saw her. That's why I pursued her. Ain't that right, bro?" Dame looks at Bruno to cosign his bullshit but Bruno shakes his head.

"Don't put me in that shit," is all Bruno chooses to say on the matter.

"So, if you pursued a hoe, as you say, then what does that make you?"

"Smart," Dame answers quickly. I roll my eyes at him.

"Hey, what's going on?" Danny asks after returning from the restroom and reading the look on my face. I stare at Dame and he turns his head.

"It's nothing." Danny looks at me worriedly.

"Are you sure?"

"Yeah. I just think I'm ready to go."

***

The group quickly decides that we've all drunk too much to attempt an hour ride back to our home. Bruno suggests a hotel Downtown that has a suite big enough to compensate us all. I phone my mother to let her know that we'll be spending the night out.

"With those Devuls?" She asks, and I tell her yes. She sighs as if she doesn't agree with our decision, "OK, well y'all just be careful; and doll, don't come back pregnant."

We stand behind the guys as they follow the procedures to check-in. We hear the concierge say that the room is usually $1,500, but because it's a weekday, it's a grand.

"This part is on y'all. I dropped five-hun at the bar," Bruno says before backing away from the counter. Rochelle walks over to him and he places his arm around her.

"I drove, so I'll put $250 on it. Danny, you and Dame can take care of the rest." Richie pulls his wallet out and produces five 50's. Danny and Dame count out the remainder of the cost and slide it to the young white man. They get the keys to the penthouse suite and we all hit the elevators. We travel quietly to the 22nd floor, mainly because we've had so much to drink that we can barely stand up straight. We head to the double doors at the end of the hall and Dame uses the key to let us in.

The ladies and I gasp once we get inside. The 2,200 square foot room has far outweighed our expectations. The soft brown and light green decor give the place a comfortable, earthy feel. The bar is fully stocked, and the bedrooms are decked out with elegant, plush linen and large personal bathrooms. We walk around sightseeing until we're satisfied.

"Guys, this suite is the bomb," Rochelle says more to Bruno than to anyone else. Tanisha and Pam nod their heads as if they agree.

"Yeah, but I only counted three bedrooms. How are we going to divvy up the sleeping spaces?" I question genuinely.

"Well, all that I know is I put almost $400 on this room so I'm getting me a bed."

"Me, too," Danny agrees with Dame.

"Shit, sorry bro, but I put $250 on it, so I claim the third one," Richie says while looking at Bruno. He and Rochelle glance at each other.

"Well, I guess we'll be on the pullout couch-"

"With me!" Tanisha adds before Rochelle can finish her statement. Tanisha smiles sexily at Bruno but Rochelle blocks it.

"Bitch! Don't even try it! Bruno is mine tonight." Dame chuckles with a shake of his head.

"See! What'd I tell ya?"

I suck my teeth at his comment, "Takes one to know one." Dame glances at me like he doesn't like the comparison.

"Anyway! Let's turn in, shall we," Bruno interjects quickly. I can tell by his tone that he's tired of hearing us go back and forth about the subject.

"Wait! No! Come on, guys. We are a bunch of fine ass people inside of an expensive ass room with a full bar and only a few hours left till checkout. We should party some more." Tanisha throws a proposition at us that is neither feasible nor appealing.

Shay shakes her head quickly, "Nish, girl, are you insane? It's three in the morning and we just drank three fifths! I seriously think that we should quit while we're ahead." Tanisha pouts.

"Shay, we're on vacation! We're supposed to be reckless and wasted! Come on, y'all. Stop being squares!" We all look at each other but no one comments on her request. She rushes over to the bar and grabs three shot bottles, "Come on, someone dare me to drink all three of these at once." We stare at her but everyone still remains silent. She looks discouraged. "Seriously guys, dare me! If you don't, I'll just keep asking all night-"

"Dammit, Tanisha, I dare you." Rochelle finally says in an unwilling tone. Tanisha smiles with satisfaction. She cracks all three bottles and forces them inside of her mouth at the same time. She tilts her head back violently and takes the spirits to the throat, damn near choking to death afterwards. Everyone laughs at her misfortune. She coughs until she regains her composure.

"Ha ha ha… very funny." She wipes the tears from her eyes, "Now, it's my turn. Rochelle, truth or dare?" Rochelle makes a surprised face as if she didn't see where Tanisha's little show was going. Rochelle lets out an irritated sigh, "Come on… I'm not going to stop pressing the issue, so you might as well answer the question."

"Dare!" Rochelle yells out after folding her arms. A sinister grin appears on Tanisha's face.

"I dare you to suck Bruno's huge dick right there on the couch." Everyone looks stunned by Tanisha's ridiculous request. Rochelle and Bruno both shake their heads in disbelief.

"Have you lost your damn mind? You think I'm about to suck his dick in front of everyone?"

"Yup, or you'll have to take a shot." Rochelle's aggravation grows.

"I'm not drinking anymore fucking alcohol. I'd vomit."

"Well don't! All you have to do is put his dick in your mouth, even if it's just for a second." Rochelle looks at Bruno with an uneasy expression and he humps his shoulders.

"Everyone has seen it already anyway, so it don't matter to me." Bruno sits on the couch and looks up at Rochelle. She hesitates, then walks slowly over to him. She gets on her knees in front of him and my eyes widen.
I know she's not actually about to go through with this shit!

"Rochelle! What are you doing?! Don't let Tanisha pressure you into some bullshit!" I exclaim. Tanisha smacks her lips at me.

"Oh, shut up, party pooper! If you don't want to play, simply take your lame ass into one of those bedrooms." I fix my mouth to respond, but Rochelle is already unbuckling Bruno's pants. She digs inside to grab his penis, but it's so massive that he has to help her maneuver it. He frees it from his underwear and Rochelle wastes no time wrapping her hand around its shaft. Everyone stares at her in anticipation, even me. She licks its fat head before taking it in her mouth.

"OOHHH!" The room roars with shocking approval. Rochelle slides her mouth down his dick, and then up again. She keeps going to the same rhythm until it grows in size and width. She struggles to get her mouth around it after a few minutes.

"Fuck, Bruno. You're choking me," she admits after plucking his hard dick from her mouth. He jerks it while biting his bottom lip.

"Damn baby, it was just getting good, too." She grins at him.

"Don't worry. I promise, by the time we leave here in the morning, you'll be satisfied." Dame smiles wide at his brother.

"Hell yeah! Now this is the type of fun I'm talking about! Rochelle, it's your turn. Who's next?"

CHAPTER THIRTEEN

Rochelle picks Dame's overly eager ass next and of course he chooses dare. He's super hyped up until she dares him to eat Tanisha's pussy.

"No! Fuck that shit! I'll do anything else but that." Tanisha, Shay and I laugh obnoxiously at his outburst but Pam looks very upset.

Tanisha walks over to him, "Naw, don't act like that now. I made you cum twice, so now it's your turn to do the pleasing." Dame shakes his head, no, adamantly.

"Please, just let me do Pam instead. I'd tongue fuck the shit out of her." Dame looks at Pam and she looks like a deer caught in headlights. Rochelle instantly disagrees with the switch.

"Sorry Damien, but there are no substitutions!" He walks towards the bar.

"Fuck it then, I'll take a shot, cause I ain't putting my mouth on her."

"Fuck you, Dame! What are you trying to say?" Tanisha shouts after reactivating her drunkenness with those three shots she just had.

"That you're a-"

"Damien!" I scream before he gets a chance to call my friend a whore again. Everyone looks at me, "What you said was a good idea. Maybe you should do Pam instead." I look over at my stepsister and she shakes her head with fear. Rochelle looks at me crazily.

"Uhh… no. My turn, my call."

"You know what, Chelle, it's cool. If he doesn't want to do that to me, then don't make him. I'm over it," Tanisha says, sounding somewhat defeated by his protests. Rochelle takes a deep breath.

"You know what? Fine. Dame, I dare you to give Pam some head." All eyes focus on Pam and she takes a nervous step back.

"I- I don't know about this." Dame walks over to her and grabs her by the hand.

"Come on, just let me. Don't be shy. I promise, you'll love me after it."

"She loved you before it. Everyone knows that she has the hugest crush on your bogus ass," Tanisha slurs out nastily. Pam's face becomes flushed with embarrassment.

Ignoring Tanisha's outburst, he leads Pam to the nearest bedroom, "How about this, we can get in the bed and I'll do it there." He pulls her into him swiftly and she panics. He leans in to kiss her passionately. She looks uptight until his tongue enters her mouth. She squeals with surprise before finally closing her eyes and enjoying the kiss.

"I'm shocked that your little vane ass brother didn't just take a shot instead of going through with this," I whisper in Danny's ear.

"Honestly, me, too. I don't know… he must really like Pam."

Dame backs Pam towards the bed without removing his lips from hers. She leans back on it once she feels it against her butt. Dame grabs her around her waist and lifts her up on the king size sleeper. He removes his shirt and gets on his knees, "Lay back for me."

We all step closer to the open door to watch Dame in action. He readjusts his hat backwards on his head before spreading Pam's legs gently. I feel so wrong for looking, but I just can't help myself.

And I ain't gonna lie… Dame is sexy as fuck!

"Girrrl… do you see how good that motherfucka looks on his knees like that?" Shay whispers to me so that no one else can hear. I bite my finger while shaking my head in agreement.

He kisses both of Pam's thighs before sliding his hands underneath her dress to grab her underwear. He slides her lace thongs down her legs slowly and tosses them to the floor. Her legs fall open as she watches him like a hawk. He looks up at her, smiling slightly before sticking his tongue between her pussy lips.

"Uhh!" She lets out a quick moan before covering her mouth rapidly. Dame makes slurping sounds on her clit, causing Shay and I to elbow one another in amazement. Dame laps at her with long licks and Rochelle looks back at Shay and I.

"Hell, I should've dared him to eat me instead!" Bruno cuts his eyes at her. Damien's head shakes like a pitbull while he nibbles on Pam's clit. She tosses her head from side to side like a crazy woman and Tanisha laughs.

"Can't handle it, can you girl? I would've been grinding all over that tongue." Damien stops licking Pam's pussy and turns around to look at Tanisha. He gives her an ugly facial expression as if she fucked up his concentration.

"Dame, you can stop whenever you want. You just had to do it for a few minutes," Tanisha reminds him. Dame looks at Pam laying sexily on the bed and licks her flavor off of his lips. He stands to his feet and flips her over like a hamburger on a grill.

"Arch your back." Dame gets back on his knees and starts eating Pam from the back. Shay, Rochelle, and I walk away from the door as if we're blown away.

"10's across the motherfucking board!" Rochelle exclaims before we hurry our nosy asses back towards Dame's room. We catch a glimpse of him eating her ass and Shay damn near faints.

"Oh Lawd! And he eats ass?" Shay places her hand on her forehead. Pam tries her best not to moan but with Dame's skill, that's nearly impossible to avoid. He attacks her clit with his tongue and she finally shouts out in bliss.

"There you go," Dame stops eating her to mumble. He flicks at her clitoris again, causing her legs to shake uncontrollably.

"Oh shit, Dame! Don't stop!"

"Mmhmm," he moans while sucking on her clit.

"Fuck, Dame! Fuck!" Pam forces her face into the bed and cums all over his face. He sticks his tongue inside of her and fucks her hard with its length.

"Damn, bro." Richie says with a shake of his head. "You're trying to outdo me now." Shay's ears perk up.

"Wait a minute… you eat ass, too?" Richie smirks at Shay.

"You wanna find out?" Shay gets giddy with excitement.

"Hell yeah!" Richie takes Shay's hand and they disappear into another bedroom.

Bruno looks at Rochelle, "So, are you ready to pick up where we left off?" Rochelle licks her lips.

"Well, do you eat pussy as good as your brother?" Bruno chuckles.

"Come on, girl. That's my little brother. I taught him everything he knows."

Rochelle grins with intrigue, "OK. Let the couch bed out then, big daddy." Bruno walks towards the sofa and Rochelle smiles at me with anticipation.

"Amber, I'm about to get all up on that thang! If you hear me screaming, don't be concerned. I'm planning on handling that giant motherfucka like a big girl tonight." Her facial expression goes sour suddenly, "As long as I can keep Tanisha's irritating ass away from us." I notice Tanisha passed out while standing against the wall and I giggle.

"I don't think you have to worry about that. Her ass is done with." I point to her and Rochelle sees what I mean. She walks over to her, leads her to a recliner in the corner, and sits her down. Tanisha is so drunk that she's barely conscious.

Rochelle reclines the chair for her and then rejoins me, "Yeah, I think you may be right."

Danny walks up to us and places his arm around my waist, "Dame just pulled out a condom and closed the door. They're about to get it in-"

"We all are," Rochelle informs him. He nods his head as if he knows that already. "Goodnight," Rochelle exclaims quickly after realizing that Bruno is done getting the bed situated. She slides off her shoes before laying next to him.

I stare at Danny, "Speaking of condoms, do you have any this time?" He smirks while pulling a stack of Magnums from his pocket.

"Oh yes, baby. I brought several. It's about to go down."

CHAPTER FOURTEEN

You would think we were shooting a porno with the constant moaning going on all morning long. Thankfully, the penthouse suite sits by itself so there are no neighbors to complain about the noise.

The Devul brothers are like chocolate energizer bunnies. Every time one gets done fucking, another one picks up where his brother left off. If I didn't know any better, I would think they were competing with each other. Danny and I are wrapping up our last round when someone knocks at the door.

"I tried to give y'all a chance to finish before disturbing y'all, but checkout is in 20 minutes." Richie's voice vibrates through the door.

"20 minutes?!" Danny and I both shout out in unison. We look at the digital alarm clock on the nightstand and realize that it's almost 11 o'clock.

"Fuck! All of us have literally been up all night! How is Richie going to drive that hour back home?" I inquire in a worried tone. Danny climbs out of bed and throws on his underwear.

"I don't know, but we'll figure it out. Even if we have to swap every 15 minutes, we'll make it work."

I jump out of the bed to get dressed as well. I throw on my dress quickly but say fuck those heels. We open our room door to find Rochelle and Shay trying their best to wake Tanisha up. They look at me with distraught faces once I walk over to them.

"This bitch is still passed out drunk! She won't get up," Shay says in a panicky tone. The guys look at each other and Bruno sighs loudly.

"I'll carry her," he mutters, tossing her over his shoulder like it's nothing. We guard her head as he walks out the door with her.

The woman behind the front desk stares at us with a puzzled look on her face when she spots four barefoot ladies and an unconscious one. We walk sluggishly through the hotel lobby. Dame slams the room keys on the counter without saying a word to her.

"Umm, Ha-Have a nice day!" She shouts out at our backs as the sliding doors close behind us.

We wait for Richie to pull the truck around and then we all climb in, sitting in the same spots we were in before. Bruno secures Tanisha's seat belt before closing the passenger side door. He jumps in last and we pull off.

"You good, Richie Rich? You need us to help you drive?" Danny asks his brother. Richie yawns before answering.

"Naw, I'm good. I'm just about to stop and grab an energy drink right quick."

Richie pulls in a gas station a short while later and parks his Suburban. He opens the driver door, "Does anyone need anything?"

"Water-"

"Aspirin-"

"Tylenol-"

"Coffee." We all say different things.

Richie looks at his brothers, "You heard your ladies. Get y'all asses out the whip and get what they asked for." The brothers don't seem too happy about having to get out of the truck. They walk slowly towards the gas station's entrance and we watch them until they disappear inside of the store.

'Girrrl...last night-"

"Bitch, tell me about it!" Shay and Rochelle exclaim while bouncing around excitedly. They obviously couldn't wait for the chance to talk about their experiences.

Pam shakes her head blissfully, "That was the best night of my life."

"So it's safe to say that you had fun your first night in the city, then?" Rochelle asks Pam facetiously. Pam giggles.

"Yes! It was so fucking amazing," she answers, drifting off into space after words. I look at her curiously. *Is this heiffa in love already?*

"Shit, we know it was! We saw half of it!" Shay teases, referring to Dame serving her up in front of everyone. She disagrees with Shay quickly.

"Oh no, you didn't see half of it. You didn't even see a fourth of it. Dame was…" She stops talking and drifts off into space again. The girls and I make interested faces.

"Wait a minute… so what you're trying to tell us is that what we saw him do wasn't his best trick?" Pam shakes her head no at my question.

"Hell no, not even by a long shot." Our eyes get big at her declaration. We all look at each other and then back at her.

"Well don't just sit there, sis! Details!" Rochelle says eagerly. Pam starts to tell it all but the truck doors open up.

"OK, ladies, we got what you asked for," Dame says, handing Pam a water. She thanks him before cracking it and taking a sip.

"Can I have a swig of that, sis? I need to take these pills,"Rochelle questions, referring to the aspirin that Bruno just handed her. She reaches for the bottle. Pam hands it to her and Rochelle takes a gulp of it.

"Thanks," Rochelle mumbles while handing it back to her. Dame puts his arm around Pam before leaning back and closing his eyes.

"Alright, y'all. We'll be home before you know it," Richie proclaims before pulling out of the gas station. Everyone else in the truck is fast asleep before he even makes it to the expressway.

***

I get out of bed for the first time that doesn't have to do with the bathroom at six o'clock the next morning. Even though I've been asleep on and off for 18 hours, I still manage to get up before any of the other ladies do.

"That must've been one hell of a trip to Atlanta for all of y'all to come home and sleep an entire day away," ma blurts out when I walk into the kitchen. I look in the fridge for some orange juice.

"Yeah. We partied harder than I've partied in a while. I don't think I'm going to do that again any time soon." My mom nods her head at me as if she wants to pry further. I turn my back to her to grab a glass from the cabinet.

"So, where did you guys sleep?" I secretly roll my eyes.
Here we go.

"We stayed at this nice hotel in Downtown Atlanta. The name slips my mind right now, though."

"Oh, really? So, you and the girls stayed in one room and the guys were in another, or…" I turn around to face my mother. I decide to give her the answer she's looking for.

"No. We all shared a three bedroom suite and had sex all night."

"Amber! What the hell is wrong with you? Why would you say something like that to me?"

"Because, that's what you wanted to hear, isn't it? I thought that's why you were asking so many questions, because you wanted to find out if we had sex with the Devuls or not." My mom is speechless. I take a deep breath before joining her at the table.

"Look, ma. I love you, but I'm grown--- we all are, and we're going to participate in grown-up behavior from time to time." I hump my shoulders at her, "Sorry."

Pam's sudden appearance pauses our uncomfortable conversation for a second. She drags herself into the kitchen to grab a glass of water.

"Oh, hey. Good morning everybody-"

"What about you? Did you have sex all night, too?" Pam stops in her tracks as if she's seriously alarmed by my mother's question. She gawks at mom and then at me.

"Pam, it's OK. I told her what we did, and I also reminded her that we're grown, and we're more than capable of taking care of ourselves." Pam looks shook by the whole conversation. She decides to grab her a quick cup of water and leave the kitchen without saying a word. I grin at my mom before standing up from the table.

"You know, just because you're grown doesn't mean that I have to like it."

"I know, ma, but it doesn't change the fact that it's true."

CHAPTER FIFTEEN

"I can't believe you fucking told your momma that," Shay says to me in an ugly tone. I hump my shoulders and flop back on my bed.

"What did you want me to do, lie? Fuck that. We're too grown for that shit."

"No, you didn't have to lie! You just didn't have to tell her the truth! She didn't need to know that we were fucking dudes that we just met the day before! Now, she's going to think we're hoes!" Rochelle fusses at me. I shake my head at both of them.

"You are," I tease, but no one cracks a smile at my joke. I sigh at their attitudes, "How can you ever expect to be treated like an adult if you don't act like one?"

"Says the woman still living with her momma," Tanisha interjects and we all look over at her. She doesn't even look up at us while filing her nails.

"You know what, I'll let that one slide. I have to keep reminding myself that you're in a shitty mood today because Dame used you for your dick-sucking skills and then kicked your ass to the curb." Tanisha looks taken aback by my words as everyone else's jaws hits the floor. She looks like she wants to clapback but the sight of Pam makes her swallow her words.

"Anyway! We're only in town for two more nights. What should we do next?" Shay questions in an attempt to change the temperature of the room.

"I don't think there's much to do in this little ass town, honestly. I just can't believe we slept all of Wednesday away! I've been turning up for years and I don't think I've ever been so wasted that I slept an entire day before." Rochelle admits.

Shay jumps in to correct her, "Oh no, sweetie, being wasted had nothing to do with our exhaustion yesterday. Well… maybe for Tanisha, but..." Shay humps her shoulders at her and Tanisha gives her a condescending look, "But what I'm trying to say is that we all know the real reasons why we were so tired and our bodies were sore when we woke up this morning," Shay finishes, referring to us being twisted up in unnatural sex positions by the Devul brothers. Her words make us reminisce for a second, prompting huge smiles to appear on our faces. Tanisha rolls her eyes at us with envy before continuing to file her nails.

"I mean… girls… I have never," Shay confesses in awe. She exhales when she thinks about Richie spreading her butt cheeks and tongue-fucking her asshole nastily.

"Girl, me neither, and I mean that literally! Bruno's dick was so fucking fulfilling-"

"Dame's was, too. I mean, he just kept eating me and fucking me and eating me and fucking me… to the point where I lost count of what round we were on. I just kept cumming-"

"Anyway, what did we decide on doing today?" Tanisha cuts Pam off to ask the room. Pam narrows her eyes at her but lets it slide. Shay grins mischievously at the question. The first thing that comes to mind is her seeing Richie again so that she can get another helping of his chocolate loving. Tanisha shuts her down before she gets a chance to say anything, "And don't even think about mentioning those brothers, either. I think I've seen enough of them to last me a lifetime."

***

The ladies and I decide to hit the town's bowling alley to knock down a couple of pins. We promised Tanisha that we wouldn't invite the Devuls, even though we all secretly wanted to do so.

"That's actually a smart idea, Tanisha," My mom said when she overheard us talking about not including the guys. Of course ma was going to agree with that. The last thing she wants is us spending another night with the guys we can't seem to keep our hands off of.

"Ugh," I mumble after tying up the ugly ass red, green, and white bowling shoes. I stand up from my seat and stare at them like they are the most atrocious things I've ever seen. I eventually start walking around the bowling alley to find a suitable ball.

"I ain't gonna lie, this type of event has 'date night' written all over it," Rochelle acknowledges after everyone chooses their balls and places them on the ball return. Tanisha places her hand on her hip.

"I thought we all agreed that we weren't going to bring up those men while we were out tonight?"

"First of all, I didn't say anyone's name, I said we're doing some date night shit. And secondly, fuck that, you agreed to that shit, not me. If I want to talk about my vacation dick, I'm going to talk about it-"

"Amen." Shay agrees and Tanisha smacks her lips.

I decide to double down on their point, "Right. We actually like the Devuls and have a good time with them. I honestly think if you would've still had one, they'd be right here with us right now-"

"Exactly, because you were the one that invited them to Atlanta with us, remember?" Shay adds to my statement. Tanisha rolls her eyes at us.

"Whatever. I don't have one because I don't want one. I can have any one of them if I really tried." We all look at her like "Bitch, we dare you". She immediately tries to backtrack, "I said if! But I wouldn't do that to y'all. Y'all are my best friends." We turn our lips up at her as she swiftly grabs her purple ball from the stand. She tries her best to avoid any of our further dirty looks. She walks up to the lane line and prepares to throw. I sit next to Pam, who's so busy texting that she's still wearing her regular shoes.

"Are you going to play?"

"Oh! Yeah, I am. Just got a little sidetracked." She smiles hard while sitting her phone down next to her. She kicks off her Reebok's.

"Let me guess… Damien?" I inquire while she slides her foot into the left bowling shoe. She glances at me like that's a topic she's not interested in discussing with me.

"I mean, it's OK if it is. I'm not going to give you a hard time about him. He seems like he really likes you."

She smiles while tying her bowling shoe, "I think he does, too."

"So, y'all going out again?" She thinks about the question before humping her shoulders.

"We haven't really talked about that. We're too busy talking about that night at the penthouse." She smiles wide at the memory and I giggle.

"Yeah… that penthouse stunt was some wild shit. I don't think I've ever done anything like that before in my life." Pam ties her other bowling shoe and her phone goes off. She picks it up to read a message. She bites her bottom lip.

"Hey, I think I'm going to sit this game out. I'm headed to the bar to grab me something to eat," she informs me before standing up from her chair. She disappears towards the food counter without saying another word.

The girls and I get through all 10 frames with goose eggs filling up a lot of the space on our scorecards. I stare at the scoreboard, "I don't think I've ever seen numbers this pathetic in my life," I admit to the other girls. They all sit down as if they couldn't care less.

"Yeah, well… who actually bowls in real life?" Rochelle asks while checking her phone.

"You're the one that suggested this bullshit! Why suggest coming here if you can't play?"

"Because this town is a hole-in-the-wall and ain't shit to do here but sleep, get drunk-"

"And fuck," Shay adds, causing us all to laugh. I look down at Pam's shoes and realize she never returned.

"Hey girls, I'll be right back." I walk to the bar and peek inside. I don't see Pam sitting at the counter or at a table and I become worried. I turn around to walk away.

"Danny?" I say shockingly, bumping directly into him. He smiles when he sees my face.

"Hey, baby." He hugs me tightly before pecking me on the lips. We separate and I look at him confusedly.

"What are you doing here?"

"I'm looking for Dame. Have you seen him?" Danny asks, glancing around the bowling alley quickly. I shake my head no, "Man, where the fuck is this fool at? He asked me to come up here with him so that he could give Pam something, but that was a half hour ago. I don't appreciate his ass leaving me in the car that long."

"That's weird, because I haven't seen Pam in about that long, either. She walked away saying that she was about to grab something to eat, but I haven't seen her since. I'm sure they're together around here somewhere, I just don't know where."

Danny and I start walking through the bowling alley, searching for our missing siblings from one end of the building to the other. My friends notice me walking with Danny and I sigh. I know Tanisha is going to think that I invited him here even though that's not the case. They stare in our direction while whispering to each other but no one approaches us. I try my best to ignore their unpleasant looks. Danny and I continue looking for Dame and Pam until we end up back where we started from.

"Well... maybe they left," I suggest, not knowing how else to explain their disappearance. Danny disagrees.

"They couldn't have. I have Dame's keys right here." He pulls them out of his pocket to show me. I take a deep breath and put my hands on my hips.
Where the fuck could they have gone?

I stand there for a few more seconds before a lightbulb goes off in my head. I walk speedily towards the restrooms. "Where are you going?" Danny questions after deciding to follow me.

"The one place we haven't checked yet." Danny looks perplexed.

"But we searched everywhere-"

"Not everywhere," I respond quickly, approaching the bathroom area. I glance at the 'men' sign on one entrance and the 'women' sign on the other. I turn to face Danny, "OK. You check the men's room and I'll check the women's." Danny agrees before walking inside. I slowly open up the ladies' bathroom door, listening for any weird noises as I enter. I hear Dame and Pam talking in the center stall and my eyes get big.
I can't believe it! I've found them.
I quietly lean against the sink and wait for them to come out.

"I know, Dame, but this has to be the last time."

"OK baby, I got you-"

"No, Dame. I'm serious this time. Promise me." Dame sighs at her mysterious request.

"Bae, I don't understand what the big deal is. I wanted to make love to you without it again. I'm addicted to the way her wetness feels wrapped around my dick. You know you were my first time-"

"Dame, we only did that at the penthouse because you ran out of condoms. I told you then that I didn't want to have unprotected sex again and you told me you understood. Now here we are having unprotected sex two more times! We have to stop being so careless-"

"OK Pam… OK. If you don't want to do it anymore, I'll respect that." The bathroom stall unlocks and the door opens slowly. I stand upright as it swings open. Pam is pinned up against the wall and Dame is kissing her so deeply that they don't notice me standing there. They both jump out of their skin once they finally look in my direction.

"Amber!" Pam shouts, wiping Dame's slob from around her mouth. I fold my arms when Dame and I make eye contact. He kisses Pam one last time before walking past me and out of the door. He doesn't even bother to acknowledge me at all and I'm glad.

Fuck you, too, scumball.

CHAPTER SIXTEEN

"Was that Dame I just saw leave with Danny?" Shay asks before Pam and I can even make it back to our lane. Pam sits down embarrassingly and I sigh loudly.

"Of course it was." All of my friends smack their lips.

"Well… what the fuck was he doing here?" Tanisha asks in an angry tone. Pam looks up at her nastily.

"None of your fucking business!" Pam's confrontational tone takes everyone by surprise. Tanisha's blood begins to boil but Rochelle puts her hands up peacefully.

"No shade here, sis. I was just smacking my lips because I wish I would've known they were coming. I would've told you to tell them to bring Bruno-"

"Richie, too," Shay throws her man's name in the ring as well. Tanisha gets fed up and slams her ass in a seat.

"You know what? Fuck this and fuck y'all! I was just trying to have a fucking girls' night out for once and I get this type of attitude? Fuck all of this shit!" Tanisha screams more to herself than at us. She switches out her shoes quickly and carries the rented ones to the shoe rental counter. We all watch her, but no one goes after her.
I think we're all officially tired of her bullshit.

"I'm so sick of her ass! She's always doing the most!" Shay spit out angrily. Rochelle shakes her head as if she agrees.

"Tell me about it. She's just mad because she's so used to getting all of the male attention with her perfect shape and her big butt. This is the first time she's not had a guy and she can't handle it-"

"I know! My fat ass is usually the one sitting on the sidelines," Shay interrupts while slamming her hands on her hips. We watch Tanisha storm into the bar and I shake my head at her unstableness.

"Anyway, I think y'all were on to something when y'all invited Dame and Danny up here-"

"I didn't invite Danny. Actually, Dame asked him to ride with him to see Pam." Rochelle and Shay stare at me as if the details don't matter.

"Whatever. My point is, maybe we should hang with the boys tonight. I mean, I'm sure we'll have more fun being with them than bowling three point games," Rochelle states, pointing to the tragic looking scoreboard. I nod my head slightly as if I agree. Pam instantly starts texting on her phone.

"So, what do you think? Should we call them?" Shay asks eagerly. Pam looks up at her before I get a chance to answer.

"I already told Dame we were coming over. He sent me the address and told me to pull up in about 30 minutes."

***

Pam drives her brand-new, red Nissan to the address Damien gave her, which happens to be Richie's house. Even though we were tired of Tanisha's shenanigans, we still couldn't leave her stranded at the bowling alley. We walked into the bar and told her where we were going, and of course she declined. We asked how she would get back to our house and she claimed she'd figure it out. We left Richie's address with her just in case she wanted to find her way there instead, even though I'm almost sure she won't.

"Damn, Richie," I mumble as we turn into his huge driveway. His lovely, brick colonial isn't as big as our mini mansion, but it's close. It sits on the end lot of a quiet block. We spot two vehicles behind Richard's Suburban and we assume that Danny, Bruno, and Dame are already here.

"I know, right!" Shay agrees with me in an impressed tone, "This man is going to make me move down here with yo' ass in a minute!"

The ladies and I hop out of the vehicle and head towards the front door. We ring the doorbell, trying not to appear as excited as we feel. We spot shadows through the covered windows before the front door opens up a short time later. Richie stands in the doorway wearing a black beater and black basketball shorts.

"Welcome, ladies." He says in that soothing ass voice that for a minute, I forgot he had. Even though Richie's not my man, I still stare him up and down slowly. *A man that fine should always be visually admired.*

He opens the door to let us in. We walk across the threshold with Shay bringing up the rear. He grabs her as soon as she steps in. "Damn, there goes my juicy beauty," he exclaims before greeting her mouth with his. She happily allows his tongue to wrestle with hers. He feels all over her body like no one is watching and Rochelle gets a little envious.

She clears her throat, "Where are your brothers?" Richie pulls away from Shay for a second, "In the back. Just follow the sound of the music."

Shay and Richie become engulfed in each other again. Realizing that's the best answer we're going to receive, we blindly head down the house's long hallway. The music that Richard was referring to gets louder with every step we take. We hear Trey Songz mention getting naked from over the speakers right before we reach the room where the guys are hanging out.

"Ladies, what's up," Bruno utters while staring intensely at Rochelle. She blushes immediately.

"Hey, Bruno," we respond at once, noticing him and Dame holding pool sticks in their hands. They stand next to a giant pool table in the center of the floor as if they were in the middle of a game. I spot Danny behind a small bar in the corner making a drink. We make eye contact once he hears my voice, and we smile at one another.

"Who's winning?" Rochelle asks, even though I know she secretly doesn't care. She walks towards Bruno but doesn't impede his personal space.

"I am," he answers, stepping towards her as well. They begin flirting heavily with their eyes.

Dame shakes his head, "So, I'm assuming this means we won't be finishing our game, then?" Bruno looks over at his little brother.

"Like you wanted to, anyway. I was tearing you a new asshole." Dame sighs as if it's true, even though he doesn't want to admit that it is.

He lays his stick across the pool table, "Whatever. I was just warming up."

Bruno ignores his brother's words and lays his pool stick across the pool table as well. Bruno moves closer to Rochelle but doesn't touch her. Their bodies are an inch away from each other with an intense energy sparking between them both.

"So, why haven't I heard from you since Richie dropped us off after we left the penthouse?" Rochelle inquires, trying her best not to sound like his absence has upset her. He allows her to linger in suspense for a second, taking in her long body from top to bottom before answering.

"The same reason why I haven't heard from you, I guess." Rochelle sucks her teeth at his answer. They stare each other down like it's the wild, wild west. I shake my head at their charade.

They clearly like each other, they just don't want the other person to know it.

Dame approaches Pam, "Just couldn't get enough of me, I see," he says jokingly. She smacks her lips and hits him in the chest.

"Oh, hush. I'm only here because the girls wanted to see your brothers. Please Damien, don't flatter yourself." He smiles at her sweetly and grabs her around the waist. He kisses her like he's been dreaming of her lips all day, even though they just saw each other at the bowling alley.

As much as I hate to admit it, Dame seems like he really likes my sister.

I walk towards Danny as he finishes making a second drink. He pushes it towards me, but I frown my face up at it. He looks at the beverage weirdly.

"What? You don't like rum and Coke?"

"No, I don't like that terrible ass hangover I had after our Atlanta trip." He nods his head slowly as if he understands. Dame walks over to us and grabs my drink from in front of me.

"I got you," he remarks, downing the beverage all at once. He slams the glass down on the bar before heading towards Pam again.

"Thanks," I exclaim facetiously. Danny picks up on my tone.

"I know he's an asshole, but he means well. Don't let that incident with Tanisha define who he is. He is a womanizer, but he's a good person in other ways. Try to give him a chance." I take a deep breath.

I can't lie... Tanisha ain't exactly innocent herself.

Pam sits on Dame's lap on a leather couch near the bar as Richie and Shay finally walk in the room to join us. They wipe their mouths as if they've been making out heavily the entire time they've been away. He holds her close to him like he never wants to let her go. She smiles ecstatically, making me so happy for my friend.

I wish she lived down here with us. Her and Richie would make a really cute couple.

"Speaking of Tanisha, where is she?" Danny asks me, bringing my attention back to him. I sigh at the question.

"At the bowling alley still, all in her feelings." He looks at me like he wants to know more, but he doesn't inquire. I decide not to volunteer anymore details, either. *I honestly don't want to talk about her anyway. I've given her drama enough of my energy.*

"So, even after what happened at the suite, you girls still wanted to party with us again, huh? I knew y'all were some freaks!" Damien exclaims with his tongue out. Pam elbows him.

"Please! It had nothing to do with the penthouse, we just wanted to see y'all again before we left town," Shay lies, looking up at Richie. He stares at her as if he's going to be a little bothered to see her go.

"When y'all leaving?" Bruno asks Rochelle. He finally wraps his arms around her, and she tries her best not to blush.

"First thing Sunday morning." The Devuls look at each other.

"Damn. Well, I guess we gotta make sure we enjoy each other until then," Richie states. Rochelle and Shay both gaze at their beaus.

"You're right, but how do we do that?" Shay questions. The room gets quiet. Everyone looks at each other cluelessly. Dame finally breaks the silence.

"Bros, remember that routine we made up when we were younger when we all thought we were gonna be strippers?" The girls and I giggle at his random outburst. Richie, Bruno, and Danny chuckle as well.

"Dame, where the fuck did that memory come from?" Bruno asks, acting like he forgot all about that.

"I still wanted to be a stripper up until about last year. I secretly practiced that dance we made up all the time. I used to be in my bedroom killing that shit." The room fills with laughter. Dame laughs, too. "Aye, don't sleep on ya boy! I know I would've got paid!" We all shake our heads at him. He slides Pam off his lap and stands up to join his brothers. "Anyway, the music is already playing, the mood is right… I was just thinking that we could maybe put on a little show for the ladies. You know, put our stripping theories to the test… just for fun?" The brothers look uneasy about the idea, but our eyes grow with excitement.

Danny looks uninterested, "I don't know about that, Dame-"

"Come on. Actually, that sounds like a great idea." I cut him off to say.

"Yeah, I agree with Amber. Show us what ya got, Devuls!" Shay adds.

"Plus, I got singles…" Rochelle exclaims, reaching in her purse and pulling out a knot of one-dollar bills. I look at her strangely.

"Chelle, why the hell are you carrying around so many singles?" I must ask.

"I collect them. You just never know when you might need to hit a vending machine, give someone change for a $20, or…" she stares at the Devul brothers, "Tip a group of fine ass men that want to try out their stripper moves on you." Everyone in the room laughs again. Dame glances at his brothers eagerly.

"So… shall we?" They look at each other before eventually nodding their heads, yes. The girls and I cheer happily. The men shake their heads with nervous grins. "OK, I'm going to set the chairs up for you ladies to sit in, and then we'll go and get prepared. I hope y'all are ready for the routine that we used to call 'These Devul D's'."

CHAPTER SEVENTEEN

Rochelle, Shay, Pam, and I sit about four feet away from each other in the black fold-out chairs that Dame got from behind the bar. We got comfortable in them while the guys picked up the heavy ass pool table and carried it to the opposite side of the room. Richie, Danny, and Bruno swallowed a few shots of liquor to calm their nerves. Then, they disappeared down Richie's hallway without saying another word to us. Now, we've been sitting in these seats for over 20 minutes and we're starting to get a little antsy.

"This better be one hell of a show," Rochelle breathes out while repositioning herself in the uncomfortable chair.

Shay folds her arms, "Tell me about it. I mean, what the fuck are they doing?"

"Probably practicing. Everyone seemed to have forgotten all about the routine when Dame mentioned it. He probably had to refresh their memory," Pam theorizes. I nod my head as if that makes sense.

"Well, they need to hurry up, because in a minute, I'm-"

BOOM!

We all jump when a sound effect coming from the speakers cuts Rochelle off. The lights dim in the room. We look around at each other frantically.

This is it!

"*Slowly*" by Tank begins playing over the speakers. We smile big with intrigue while staring at the room's entrance.

I've always thought this song was sexy!

The song's intro vibrates the floor as Tanks's high-pitched adlibs make us dance modestly in our seats. Rochelle quickly hands each lady a handful of singles, keeping a nice amount of them for herself. We count them out of habit, but a body appearing in the doorway quickly snatches our attention away from the money. Dame stands there wearing red jogging pants, wheat colored Tim's, and a black fitted hat pulled down low. He looks down at his chest, flexing his oiled-up muscles to the beat of the song.

"WOOO!" We cheer him on. He walks in the room intensely, stopping right before he fully reaches Pam.

"Set the mood..."

Tank begins singing seductively. Dame starts to roll his body alluringly while rubbing his hands down his chest. His body moves precisely to the beat, making me bite my lip at how sensual he looks. His hands continue sliding down south into the top of his pants. He strokes his dick with both palms, causing Pam to fan herself with the one-dollar bills.

"Come on in..."

Dame gets on his knees and slides towards Pam, spreading her legs in a quick, aggressive motion. Her eyes open wide with surprise. Dame acts like he's eating her, burying his face in the crotch of her denim shorts. She squeals with amusement as another Devul appears at the door.

"Slowly, I know..."

Bruno stands in the doorway, providing us with the silhouette of a perfect male specimen. He and Dame are dressed the same, except Bruno's sweats are navy blue instead of red. He raises up both arms and flexes his loaded guns like a strong man at a bodybuilding competition. His shiny muscles are extremely defined, making Rochelle wiggle excitedly in her seat.

Bruno walks in provocatively with his eyes set on Rochelle. She swallows nervously from the power behind his stride. He stands between her legs, forcing her to stare right at the one thing she used to be so afraid of…
His long cock.
His skin fills her nose with the aroma of coconut oil. He leans down and puts his face within inches of hers. "Give me your hands." She raises them anxiously and he grabs them with his.
"Slip it off, yeah…"

He slides her hands steadily down his rock-hard stomach while gyrating to the beat. Her fingers trace all eight of his abs before he affixes her hands around the top of his pants. She tugs down on them slowly, revealing his man bush and then the start of his huge dick. His thick meat is bent down beautifully, looking like the start of a giant slope that any woman would be lucky to slide down.
"Really, really want to take my time…"

Richie appears in the doorway next, rocking his black joggers low on his hips. His black Timberland boots are untied, and his black hat sits on his head backwards. He sways his body side-to-side in a sexy way, looking like he's no stranger to the art of exotic dancing.

"Shit," Shay mumbles with a bite of her lip. The oil covering his body makes his skin resemble a black river underneath the moonlight. His muscles look like they've been perfectly crafted by the gods if I do say so myself.
"Slowly, I know…"

He rolls his way towards Shay. She holds her hands out for him before he even reaches her. He takes them in his and places them on his shoulders once he gets on his knees in front of her. He whispers something in her ear, and she giggles.
"Slowly, I know…"

The chorus starts over again and I stare at the doorway. *"It should finally be my turn,"* I say excitedly to myself. A few seconds later, my wish comes true. Just like his brothers that came before him, Danny dramatically comes into view. His jogging pants are gray and just like Richie's, they hang low on his hips. He fondles himself vulgarly until the chorus comes to an end.
"Come on in! Close the door!..."

Danny slams the door shut behind him and all the men quickly meet him in the middle of the floor. They perform a well-choreographed, sexually explicit routine that has us going wild. They roll their bodies to the floor before humping the ground nastily. Dame works the floor with fast pumps, sticking his tongue out once he slows it down.

"Ok, Pam!" Rochelle gives Pam props after catching a glimpse of Dame's rhythmic skills. Pam smiles proudly at her man's performance.
"Making love, all through the night! Slowly..."

The brothers slide towards their respective dates and freestyles the remainder of the routine. Dame snatches Pam up from her chair. He picks her up and flips her upside down in a 69 position. Bruno helps Rochelle up from her seat and bends her pornographically over her chair. Richie picks Shay up with ease and wraps her legs snugly around his waist, while Danny sucks on my inner thigh like he's trying to give me a passion mark.

The song comes to an end and the brothers release us. They take a step back and we all clap loudly for them.

"Bra-fucking-vo!" Shay exclaims, throwing her singles at Richie.

"Yasss daddy!" Rochelle shouts, throwing her singles at Bruno as well.

"Mmm… that was so good," Pam compliments Dame while walking up to him and placing the money in his pants. I don't say anything with my mouth, but my eyes tell Danny everything he needs to know. I approach him to stick the singles all over his wet chest. Every Devul smiles proudly.

"Glad you liked it," Dame forces out slightly winded. He wipes the sweat from his brow, "So, do you think we have a future in stripping?" We laugh at his question.

Pam speaks up before anyone else can, "Yes you do, as long as it's only for me."

CHAPTER EIGHTEEN

The fellas made us so hot and bothered with their sexy dance moves that now we can't seem to keep our hands off them. We make out with them in the middle of the room while our fingertips constantly feel all over their chocolate muscles.

"You betta stop rubbing on me like this before something happens," Bruno warns Rochelle. She smirks at his statement.

"Please?" He shakes his head at her.

"You so nasty."

She leans in to kiss his lips again, "I know." She leads Bruno to the chair she was sitting in and forces him to sit down. She looks over at us, "It's our turn, ladies. Let's give our men a treat." We stare at her confusedly but Richie, Danny, and Dame look excited by the suggestion. They join their brother in our old seats expeditiously. We give Rochelle unenthused looks until she walks over to us, and we huddle together.

"Girls, I want that man so fucking bad," she admits before looking at Bruno lustfully.

I smack my lips at her, "OK, so what?! What the fuck does that have to do with us?!" I whisper angrily. *She knows that I can't dance!*

She smacks her lips back at me, "What the hell do you mean, 'What does that have to do with you'? Ain't that our men sitting right there?" She glances at them and I do, too.

"Yeah...and…"

"AND they just did something so fucking hot for us. We should do something hot for them."

"Bitch, you know I'm not about to get my big ass up in front of everyone and do a striptease," Shay comments quickly. Rochelle shakes her head as if we're not getting it.

"No! No one said anything about dancing."

"So, what is it that you had in mind, then?" Pam asks interestingly. Rochelle smiles naughtily.

"How about we hold a competition?"

"What type of fucking competition?" Shay snaps with her eyebrows raised.

"We should see who can make our man cum the quickest." Everyone's face becomes flushed with confusion, but we're too speechless to ask her to clarify. She smacks her lips, "Come on, y'all. It'll be fun."

"You know what, you're acting real Tanisha-ish right now." Pam and Shay giggle at my comparison but Rochelle doesn't find it funny.

"Look, this whole vacation has been incredibly raunchy! Since we've been here, we've met, sucked, and fucked men that we just met! We might as well go out the same way we came in."

"I don't know about this-"

"Yeah. me, either." Pam agrees with me. Rochelle turns to address us both.

"Look, I get it, y'all live here, so I'm really not talking to y'all. I'm more so talking to Shay." Shay makes a face as if she's unsure. "You could always do it in his bedroom, but where's the fun in that? You already saw me give Bruno some head. It's really nothing to it."

"What the hell are y'all about to do, play football?" Dame asks us impatiently. We glance at him with narrow eyes before engaging with each other again.

"So, what'll it be?" We look at one another before taking a deep breath. Shay agrees to it first, followed by Pam. I look at Pam shockingly and she humps her shoulders.

"Well, he did it to me in front of everyone."

"That's the spirit!" Rochelle exclaims, praising Pam's terrible decision. The women walk towards the seated men without me.

"I'm in," I say at the last minute. I join them while they're standing in front of the guys. The fine brothers look up at us and I sigh to myself.
Well Amber, here goes nothing.

***

The Devuls' jogging pants rest around their ankles as each woman places their heads in their laps. Rochelle goes to work on Bruno's penis out the gate, showcasing her extreme comfort with sucking his dick in front of everyone.

"Fuck… that's it, baby," Damien moans, rooting Pam on as soon as her mouth wraps around his love stick. He holds her braids in his fists so that he can get a better look of her slurping on his cock.

"Aww...Sss…" Richie moans out in a low tone. Shay gobbles his meat up like a carnivore. Her lips fit around his penis so snuggly that her drool barely runs down his shaft. I stroke Danny's dick with my hand while looking over at everyone else. I watch them in action, feeling completely weirded out by us agreeing to do this.

He stares down at me, "You know, you don't have to do this if you don't want to." His face is genuine with his words. He glances over at everyone else as if he's secretly envious of their pleasure. I decide that I don't want to disappoint him and take his penis in my mouth. I start sucking him shyly at first, but I eventually get into it.

"Damn, baby. That feels good," he notes joyfully. I use his verbal confirmation as a confidence booster and suck him faster. "Shit!" He shouts. The other ladies hear about my well-doing and step their slurping up.

"Gotdamn! Fuck… Aye bros, I think I like this game," Dame expresses in between moments of bliss. The men hear him acknowledging them, but they are too busy enjoying their own pleasure to respond.

"Just like that, beautiful… You're gonna make me cum," Richard informs Shay with heavy breaths. She keeps up her pace, taking his entire length down her throat like her gag reflex doesn't exist. "Oh… Ohh… OHH SHIIIT!" Richie roars out. His pelvis jerks upward when he cums hard down her throat. The rest of us remove our man's dicks from our mouths and smack our lips in defeat. Shay swallows his creamy center before sliding her lips off him.

"Fuck, Shay! I think I love you." Everyone stops and stares at Richie as if our ears have deceived us. He pulls up his pants quickly, sporting a look as if he's slightly embarrassed.

"Wait a minute, Rich… What did you just say to me?" He stands up in front of her while helping her to her feet as well. He smiles sweetly at her.

"Shay, this week has been so fucking amazing for me. I've never met a woman as caring, well-rounded, and funny as you. I don't have any complaints whatsoever-"

"Not even about my weight?" She asks self-consciously. He stares at her as if he doesn't understand what she means.

"Why do you keep talking about your weight like it's a bad thing? Do you really think your size is a negative?" She humps her shoulders at his question, but what she really wanted to say was yes. "Look, I like my women with curves. Honestly, the more, the better. You are so fucking gorgeous to me, and I wouldn't change a thing about you." Shay blushes harder than she's ever blushed before. Richie takes her in his arms.

"So, you think you love me?" He smiles wide at her inquiry.

"What I think is that we have the makings for a beautiful relationship that could cause me to fall in love with you quickly. If you were around for a few more weeks, I'm sure I'd be wrapped up in you so tight that no one would be able to pry us apart." A big smile appears across Shay's face as well, followed quickly by a look of sadness.

She lays her head on Richard's chest, "Fuck, Richie! I've been waiting on a guy like you and now that I've found you, I have to leave you." He holds her tightly.

"Well, I guess that means it's not the right time for us." They hold each other lovingly without saying anything else. Rochelle, Pam and I finally get off our knees. We look at Shay with gloomy faces.

Dame looks at Pam and then at Richie and Shay. He makes an annoyed face, "OK… I get it. It's sad that Shay's leaving, but in the meantime, I need to get this cum out." Everyone gawks at him with disgusted facial expressions, but he ignores us, "Pam, let's go upstairs. I have a game of my own that I want us to play."

CHAPTER NINETEEN

Bruno, Dame, and Danny stand up to fix their pants. Damien walks towards the door, grabbing Pam's arm on the way past her. She snatches away from him.

"Dame! What's your problem?" He turns around and looks at her with a perplexed expression.

"What's my problem? Pam, what's your problem? I told you I wanted to go upstairs-"

"Yeah, but I don't." He looks taken aback by her tone.

"How are you going to just do what you did to me, and then get an attitude when I want you to finish?" She folds her arms.

"I would finish if you weren't acting like such an ass right now." He chuckles at her attempt to insult him.

"Ass? You think I'm acting like an ass?" He laughs obnoxiously like he does when he's about to say something inappropriate. He glances at Danny and Danny frantically shakes his head no. "Naw, me being an ass would be me telling you that I only showed interest in you because Danny asked me to." Everyone's face hits the floor, including Danny's and mine. I look at Danny angrily before turning my attention back to Dame, "He told me that you were so hurt about me and Tanisha that I should be "decent" and give you some attention, so not only did I give you a little attention, I gave you this dick, too. You're welcome." Pam's eyes well up with tears, making me so furious that I can kill Dame. Rochelle steps up and puts her arm around Pam.

"You know what, Dame? You are such a fucking douchebag," Rochelle spits out while allowing Pam to cry on her shoulder. Damien humps his shoulders like he doesn't care.

"Call me whatever you want, but at least I'm not naive. I saw Pam every day in school for four years straight. If I wanted her, I would've had her by now."

"Ugh!" Shay exclaims, stepping up to comfort Pam as well. Dame turns his face up at her.

"Ugh back to you, you fat bitch."

"Dame, you're out of line now. You better quit while you still have all your teeth in your mouth." Richie warns, stepping towards his brother slowly. Dame looks shocked by Richard's words.

"Really, big bro? You're going to take up for some chick you barely know over your own brother?"

"You know what, Dame? That's your fucking problem, man. You're a disrespectful, immature little boy and you need to grow the fuck up," Richie adds aggressively. Danny steps up to confront Dame as well.

"And don't try to make it seem like I told you to talk to Pam to do her a favor. I was actually trying to do your terrible ass a favor. She's a good girl and I was hoping she would rub off on you in a positive way. Instead, all you did was try to ruin her life. I honestly should've known better. Your attitude is poisonous as fuck." Danny approaches Pam and rubs her back soothingly, "I'm so sorry, Pam. I swear, I meant well. The last thing I wanted was for you to get hurt." Dame makes an overwhelmed face as if he's being attacked. He storms out of the room without saying another word.

"I'm sorry, ladies, I really am. I didn't expect your first time coming to my crib to be this awful," Richie addresses.

"That motherfucka, Dame, man. He shole can kill a mood," Bruno adds. Pam wipes her eyes after the cancer known as Damien leaves the room.

"I'm fine. I just need a little time to myself. I think I'm going to get out of here." She takes her keys from her pocket. "You ladies need a ride back to the house?"

"Shay, I was hoping you'd stay with me a little longer. I need to apologize to you on my brother's behalf," Richie proposes to her. She grins at him.

"No need. You aren't responsible for the things he says-"

"But I am responsible for the way he makes you feel. Come on, baby, please stay. Just for a few more hours. Let me remind you that your body is perfect just the way it is." He grabs her by the hand and pulls her into him. He kisses her forehead seductively. She closes her eyes as if his smooch is the best feeling in the world.

"OK," she surrenders easily. Richard smiles with satisfaction. Bruno stares at Rochelle.

"What about you? You interested in riding with me to my place?" Rochelle acts like it doesn't matter to her, even though deep down inside she's dying to be alone with Bruno. She walks over to him, and he places his arm around her.

Danny looks at me oddly, "I know you're pretty mad at me and I know I need to make it up to you, but I rode with Dame today and my car is at his place-"

"Don't worry about it, Danny. I will just see you some other time." He smiles at me uneasily before kissing me hurriedly on the cheek. I walk towards the front entrance with Pam and Richie. We wait while he opens the door.

"Have a good night," he says to us, watching us walk towards Pam's car. We spot Dame sitting in his Monte Carlo and I roll my eyes. Pam, on the other hand, stares him down until she gets to the driver side of her vehicle. They make eye contact one last time before she starts her car and drives away.

***

Hey, doll," moms greets me when I walk in the front door. She's sitting on the couch with Tanisha in front of the TV. I come in solo and they both looked confused. "Where is everyone else?"

"Well, Rochelle and Shay are on dates and Pam said she was in the mood for a night drive-"

"And you let her go alone?"

"I didn't let her do anything, ma, she's a grown woman. I offered to go with her, but she insisted on being alone." My mother listens to my tone and decides to let the subject die. Tanisha stares straight ahead at the TV as if she doesn't want to make eye contact with me. My mom notices her attempt to avoid me and turns off the television.

"You ladies need to talk," my mother grunts out while standing up from the couch. She walks out of the room to leave Tanisha and I by ourselves. The silence gets awkward quickly. I eventually sit in the spot that my mom was sitting in.

"I'm glad you were able to make it back safely," I throw out there, deciding to break the silence between us. She plays with the sleeves of her nightgown nervously.

"Yeah. I decided to call your mom to come and get me. She was wondering why everyone left without me. I had to explain to her what was going on." I nod my head slowly, wondering if she told the truth or a convincing ass lie. She makes eye contact with me for the first time, "And yes, I told her the truth."

"And?" Tanisha takes a deep breath.

"And she told me that I needed to apologize for being so selfish."

"Well, do you think you need to apologize?" She humps her shoulders like a kid in trouble.

"I honestly don't know how I feel. The only thing I do know is that I love you gals and I don't want us fighting over nothing. Y'all are my sisters." I smile at Tanisha and she smiles as well. She leans over to hug me. "I'm sorry, Amber. I didn't mean to come down here and cause any trouble."

"Yes you did," I say jokingly. She smacks her lips and laughs.

"You're right… I did, but only in a good way."

CHAPTER TWENTY

Shay, Rochelle, Tanisha, and I sit at the kitchen table laughing over breakfast. We discuss the events that had taken place last night and Tanisha looks amazed.

"I can't fucking believe I missed all of that!" She exclaims with a shake of her head, "And I really can't believe that Dame said all those awful things about Pam! I guess I got off easy with him calling me a few hoes. Pam really didn't deserve that." Tanisha sounds sincere, surprising the rest of the group. The back door opening in the kitchen catches us off guard.

"Hey, Pam," everyone says when we see her walk in. She looks shocked to find us all sitting in the kitchen.

"Hey girls."

"Long night?" I ask her quickly. She glances at me as if she's not interested in talking about it.

"Something like that." She walks past us and heads towards the stairs. She drags her body up the steps and we hear her room door close a short time later. We look at each other with concern.

"Dame really hurt her bad, huh?" Tanisha asks and we all shake our heads yes. She sighs at our answer. "Ugh, fuck him! We should kick his ass!"

***

The girls decided to spend their last night in town getting to know my mom's new husband, Craig. We helped ma cook a huge dinner and then we all ate outside on the patio. We talked and laughed just like we used to do back in Detroit. It felt so good not having any animosity in the air for a change. I didn't want my friends leaving on a sour note. We've always had an unbreakable bond, and that will never change.

Now, we're lying on the den floor on top of a huge comforter in front of a 75 inch, flat screen TV. We laugh hysterically at some dumb comedy movie streaming on Netflix. My girls are laying on one side of me and Pam is laying on the other. I realize that Pam hasn't giggled once at the ridiculous antics of the movie's main characters. I glance in her direction. She's lying there staring at the screen, but she's obviously not processing the movie. I rock my body into hers lightly to get her attention. She makes a startled face as if I've ripped her away from a deep thought.

I lean over to whisper to her, "Hey, you OK?" She nods her head with a fake yes. I look at her like I'm serious. She sighs.

"I mean, for the most part, yeah… I'm OK." I give her a worried stare.

"Pam, what happened last night? Where were you?" She glances at me as if she did something awful. I roll my body towards her to give her my undivided attention. "Pam… seriously, you know that I'll always be here for you, right?" Tears build up in her bottom eyelids.

"Amber, I fucked up." Her words scare me. She puts her head down as if it's the end of the world, "I was such a mess last night. I was so heartbroken and angry. I could've strangled Dame! I was crying so much that my head started hurting. I just needed to feel better." She pauses to wipe the tears falling from her eyes, "You tried to tell me about him, but I didn't listen. I was too embarrassed to confide in you about my feelings after I blew up on you for simply trying to help the last time, so I didn't have anyone to talk to. I felt alone, so I called Mr. Stanson." My eyes widen with surprise. Pam looks at me as if she's afraid to keep talking.

"So, you were with Mr. Stanson last night?"

"Yeah… at a motel." She covers her face with both hands shamefully. I rub her back in a caring way.

"I mean, it's all good, Pam. Don't be so hard on yourself. You went back to him because he was familiar to you. You felt like you could trust him-"

"That's the point, I thought I could trust him, but he was just using me! He pretended like he cared about what I was going through just to get me to sleep with him! After we finished, he told me that it could never happen again and to lose his number. Amber… I- I've lost every man I've ever cared about in one night!" Pam can no longer control her emotions. Her loud talking and crying causes Tanisha, Shay, and Rochelle to tune into our conversation. They move closer to Pam to console her.

She cries freely and we all wrap our arms around her. We hold her tightly just like she's one of us.
… because she is one of us.
We finally separate and she looks at everyone embarrassingly. She giggles, "I remember a time when you three didn't like me, now you're acting like I'm a part of your clique."

"Pam, you are," Shay says sweetly. Tanisha and Rochelle nod their heads as if they agree.

"But that doesn't mean that we won't fight, and that doesn't mean that we have to like each other all of the time. It simply means that you're not alone, and we will always be here for you, no matter how far away you may be," Tanisha states, staring at me after her words as if that message was intended for me, too. We smile at each other lovingly.

Pam perks up and wipes her eyes, "Wow. I feel a little better now." Shay grins at her.

"You know what would make you feel a whole lot better? Coming in this kitchen with me and helping me make a big ass banana split that we all can share!" Tanisha and Rochelle's eyes get big at Shay's suggestion.

"Hell yeah!" Rochelle cosigns, sounding greedy as hell. We get up from the floor and head to the kitchen.

"I swear, I'm going to miss you chicks when you leave," I tell my friends after we sit down at the kitchen table to enjoy the obnoxiously sized ice cream boat. They eat spoonfuls of the cold dessert before Rochelle responds.

"We're going to miss you, too. You know, you're going to have to come back to the 'D' before the summer is out." I nod my head as if I know. We sit in silence while eating a few more scoops, "And when you come, don't forget to bring Bruno." Everyone at the table giggles.

"Speaking of Bruno, how did your date turn out? You and Shay barely said a word about Bruno or Richie when you got back." They look at each other as if they know something that we don't.

"Umm… Well, of course Bruno and I had fun. He's a lot different when no one else is around." She smiles as if that's a good thing. Shay nods her head.

"Yeah, Richie and I had a great time, too. I swear, that man is so fucking awesome. I still don't understand why he's single."

"That's a good question," I think. *"For the Devuls to be so fine, why are any of them single?"*

"So, will they be seeing us off tomorrow?" Tanisha asks, trying her best not to sound jealous.

"No. We said our goodbyes last night. We thought it would be better that way."

"Same," Shay agrees with Rochelle. I sigh as all this talk about the brothers makes Danny cross my mind. I still haven't talked to him since that Dame and Pam shit happened last night. He knew exactly how I felt about Dame and he hooked him up with Pam anyway. I just don't have anything to say to him right now. I guess he feels the same way about me.

"I think it ended how it was supposed to end. One week of being in a sexually driven relationship with one of the finest men I've ever laid eyes on... those types of situations aren't meant to last forever. We played the roles we needed to play to get through this week. We all know our feelings for these men aren't real-"

"Speak for yourself," Shay spits out quickly. "The way Richie and I feel for each other is definitely real." No one knows how to respond to that, so we get quiet again. Tanisha drops her spoon inside of the huge dish.

"I'm full. I'm headed back into the den to find something else to watch." She stands up from the table and leaves the kitchen. Pam agrees and follows her.
I look down at the bowl, "There's a lot of this shit left."
Shay stands up and grabs it.

"Let's finish this in the den with the girls. You know how Tanisha is, she's going to pick a bullshit movie that no one else wants to see and we're going to be stuck watching it. I need to intervene before she chooses." Shay carries the melting banana split while Rochelle and I follow her. We make it to the den just as Tanisha is selecting a title, "Nope! Let me see what that is first." Tanisha smacks her lips at Shay.

"Why? Y'all weren't even in here yet. I should be able to pick what I want to watch-"

"Hell no! You know how you are! I'm not watching no B-list bullshit..."

The girls start arguing and I smile to myself.
I'm really going to miss them.

CHAPTER TWENTY-ONE

Two months Later

Danny stares into my eyes as he slowly strokes my pulsating pussy with his hard dick. His teal bed sheets are drenched with our bodies' secretions. This is our fourth time going at it and I can't believe he's not tired yet. He places his forehead on mine.

"Is it mine?" I nod my head yes. He fucks me harder, "Tell me it's mine."

"It's yours, Danny!"

"Good."

He kisses me deeply. He pounds away at me, making me shake with an orgasm. I splash squirt all over his thrusting pelvis. He bathes in my juices with no complaints.

"Give me some more of that shit," he demands, speeding up his stroke to lightning speed. I cum harder than before. My squirt is out of control. My legs tremble with weakness.

"SHIT, DANNY! I CAN'T TAKE ANYMORE!" I scream out at the top of my lungs. He growls with dominance.

He loves it when he's conquering my pussy.

"Good, because I'm about to cum!" He slides in and out of me a few more times before exploding deep between my walls. He collapses his wet body on mine once he's done. "Fuck, baby! I think that was the last one." I giggle while he rolls off me. I jump up from the wet spot quickly, nearly collapsing after my wobbly legs try to give out on me. He laughs at my lack of balance.

"That's what you get for trying to run." I smack my lips at him.

"I'm not running, I just need to get in the shower. We've been at it for hours." He produces a giant smile.

"I know. You should've never told me that you got your birth control. Now, I'm going to be busting inside of you every chance I get." I frown at how nasty that sounds. He chuckles at my reaction.

"So, you still thinking about going to Detroit this weekend?" He asks my back as I head inside of his master bathroom. I turn on the shower.

"Yup. I've been missing my city lately, plus I can't wait to see my girls again." He walks into the bathroom to join me.

"Well… do you want company?" He grabs me from behind and wraps his arms around me snuggly.

"Yeah, that's why I'm going to ask Pam to go with me." He makes an offended noise and I laugh. I turn around to face him, "Of course I want you to come with me, babe. Especially since you've always wanted to visit Detroit. I can show you around." He holds me tightly while staring into my eyes.

"Aww, our first real trip as a couple." I grin at him cheekily.

"Oh, shut up. We went to Atlanta together, remember?" He shakes his head yes.

"Of course I do, but that doesn't count. We stopped talking right after that, so our relationship never got a chance to blossom. This second go-around, we've been doing great, and we're officially in a relationship now. You're my lady." He looks at me seriously and I blush. He kisses my lips.

"Well, I guess you're right. This will be our first trip as a couple. This should be fun." He releases me before stepping in the shower.

"Yup, especially since my brothers won't be around to ruin anything this time."

***

"So, Pam? What do ya think? Me, you, and Danny hopping on a plane to Detroit?" Pam continues to wash the dishes with her back facing me. I stare at her strangely, "Pam? Are you even listening to me?" I get up from the table and stand next to her at the sink. I notice tears running down her face. I quickly turn her around to face me.

"Pam! What's wrong?" She boohoos at my inquiry while laying her head on my shoulder. She cries so hard that I assume someone died. I walk her to the table where she sits down. She wipes her face hopelessly. "Pam, please talk to me." She plays with her fingers on her lap.

"Amber, something is wrong with me." Concerned, I take her hands in mine.

"What do you mean, something's wrong with you? What is it?"

"I feel awful, like I have the flu. I can't eat, I can't sleep. I'm bloated and my period is late." My eyes get frighteningly big at her confession. I slowly sit back in my seat.

"Pam, are you trying to tell me what I think you're trying to tell me?" She looks up at me with a scared expression on her face.

"I don't know for sure because I'm too afraid to take a test, but I think…" She stops talking as if her next words are too painful to escape her lips. I hug her immediately.

"Pam, everything is going to be OK. I promise. You're not alone. We can just head up to the free clinic where I get my birth control. They'll let us know what's going on."

***

Pam sits on the doctor's table in a hospital gown. Her legs shake nervously while she gawks at all the posters about feminine hygiene and childbirth stuck to the walls. She finally looks my way and I smile at her. She takes a deep breath.

"Amber, what if I'm pregnant? What am I going to do?"

"Well, whatever you wanted to do, I guess." She looks at me with a nervous expression.

"What would you do, I mean, if you were me?" I let out an overwhelming sigh. I shake my head as if I'm unsure.

"Let's just see what the doctor has to say first. Then, we'll go from there."

"Knock, knock," we hear, before the door swings open. A petite, white lady holding a clipboard walks in with a smile.

"Hello, Pamela. My name is Dr. Shire and I'll be seeing you today. How are you feeling?" She stares at Pam attentively.

"Well, I feel sick. A little light-headed, my boobs hurt like crazy. I can't sleep." The doctor nods her head as if she understands.

"Well, those are all normal signs of early pregnancy. We tested your urine, and you are indeed pregnant." Shock covers Pam's face. My face doesn't look much different. "I'm guessing this wasn't planned."

"No," Pam mumbles. The doctor places her hand on top of Pam's.

"Listen, I understand this news can be scary, but babies are a blessing! We have several resources here to aid you in making the best decision for you. What about the dad?" Pam makes a startled face at the question, so the doctor backtracks instantly, "I'm sorry. We don't have to talk about him. What's important is that you do what's best for you. Here, I wrote you a prescription for prenatal vitamins and nausea medication. They should help you feel better." Dr. Shire rips the prescription from the notepad and hands it to her. She smiles at Pam warmly, "Make sure you come back and see me in about a week. We need to do an ultrasound to see how far along you are. See the receptionist out front to set up your appointment." The doctor leaves the room before Pam can process the news. She slowly looks over at me.

"Amber, I'm pregnant."

"I know, I heard." Tears build up in her eyes, but she refuses to let one fall.

"What would you do?" She returns to the question I tried so desperately to dodge. I become speechless.

"Pam, do you honestly think you can take care of a baby right now?" She thinks hard about my question. "And what would ma and dad say?" The mentioning of our parents frightens her somewhat, "And what about Dame? I know you two were having unprotected sex, I heard y'all talking about it in the bathroom. Do you really want to have a baby by that asshole?" She makes eye contact with me. She shakes her head slowly.

"Amber, that's the problem: I don't know if Dame *is* the father." I look drastically taken aback. "Remember my one-night stand with Mr. Stanson?" My mouth falls open.

I completely forgot about that shit!

"He used a condom, I'm sure," I say hopefully.

"He did, but it broke. That's why he freaked out about us not talking again. The thought of me getting pregnant scared him straight, I guess."

"Pam, you never told me that!" She humps her shoulders embarrassingly.

"That was a detail I could've gone without telling." We stare at each other as if we don't know what to say to one another. She sighs heavily, "Well, let me get dressed and make this appointment. I don't know what I'm going to do. All that I know is that I'm ready to get the fuck out of here."

CHAPTER TWENTY-TWO

"I'm starving," Pam confesses as we walk out of the clinic doors. She clutches pregnancy pamphlets in her hand. We start walking towards her car.

"I know you are. What did the doctor say again? That you were like nine weeks pregnant?"

"Yeah, almost ten according to the date of my last period."

"Shit! That's pretty far along."

"I know, right."

"What's up, Pam?" We hear, prompting us both to turn around suddenly. Dame stands behind us awkwardly, like he's afraid of what our reactions are going to be. We both look shocked.

"H-Hello, Damien," she stutters, as if he's the last person she expected to lay eyes on right now. He approaches us slowly.

"I've been calling you," he states, maneuvering his sexiness in front of her face. She swallows hard.

"I know. I've been ignoring them." He sighs.

"Look, I'm not good at apologizing, but I was wrong… dead wrong. I want you to forgive me."

"Fine. I forgive you." He shakes his head at her facetiousness.

"I'm serious, Pam. I miss what we had." He reaches out for her hand, but she takes a step back. He glances down at her hand, "What's that?" She forgets about the pamphlets in her hands and tries to hide them. He takes them from her before she gets the chance to do so. He glances at them quickly. "Pam, are you pregnant?"

"Come on, Amber. Let's go." She turns around to walk away hurriedly. He grabs her by the arm.

"Pam, seriously. You're pregnant and you weren't going to tell me?" She snatches away from him.

"Tell you? For what? You're an awful person, Damien! I would never want that for my child!"

"Our child! I can't believe you were just going to carry around my fucking baby without telling me!" She stomps towards her car, and he follows closely behind her. I tail them both.

"Dame, I don't want to talk about this right now." She opens the driver's door but he stops her from getting in.

"We are definitely going to talk about this! What are you planning on doing?"

"Getting rid of it," she spits out quickly. I can tell she didn't mean it. Instead, she said it to hurt him. He makes a face as if she succeeded.

"So, I get no say so?"

"None whatsoever." He tightens his jaw in defeat. She tries to get in the car again but bends over to hurl instead. Dame takes a step back. Pam vomits until she feels relieved. She looks embarrassed afterward while wiping her mouth. Dame steps close to her.

"Are you OK?"

"Fine," she answers rapidly.

"When was the last time you ate?" She thinks about his question.

"I don't remember." He tries to place his hand on her stomach, but she knocks it away. He sighs.

"Come on, at least let me feed you. I'm not about to let you starve my child."

***

    I stand outside the restaurant across the street from the clinic. Dame and Pam went inside to eat, but I didn't want any parts of their situation. I wait impatiently for Danny to pull up. He finally does and I jump inside of his car. He looks at me weirdly.

"What happened?" He asks, reading my face.

"Nothing. I just needed a ride home."

"How did you get to the clinic if you didn't drive?"

"I rode with Pam." He looks confused.

"Rode with Pam?"

"Yeah… she's going through something right now. I'm supporting her." Danny listens to my response and decides to mind his own business. After he used what I told him about Pam liking Dame in a catastrophic way, I decided to keep other people's business, especially Pam's, to myself.

    Danny drops me off at home and I thank him. I sit in the kitchen having a cocktail, deciding to wait for Pam to come home. Pam walks in the back door about an hour and a half later.

    Her eyes land on me immediately, "Hey, sis."

    "Hey," I say eagerly, perking up once she sits down to join me. She looks at me while sighing.

    "What a day." She sits her purse on the table.

    "I know… are you OK?" She nods her head yes.

    "Dame spent our whole lunch date trying to convince me to keep this baby."

    "Well, did you tell him that the baby might not belong to him?" Her eyes get big at the thought.

    "Hell no! I could never!" I look at her uneasily.

    "But don't you think he deserves to know?"

    "No! Especially if I'm not keeping it." I make a disagreeing face with her, and she rolls her eyes at me, "Amber, please don't start. I thought about it, and I decided I can't do this. I mean, I'm only 21 for god's sake! I haven't even figured out what I'm going to do with my life yet! Plus, the father options are Dame and Ronald. That's a shitty deal for my baby either way and you know it." She shakes her head and so do I. A knock at the door pauses our conversation.

"Who is it?" I shout before reaching for the doorknob. I open the door before I get an answer.

"Shay?!" I yell shockingly. Pam stands to her feet once she hears who it is and hurries over to join me, "What are you doing here?"

Shay smiles awkwardly while sitting her suitcases down, "I've decided to move down here to give Richie and I a chance. Surprise, ladies! I'm moving in!"